AWAKEN

SKYE MALONE

PRONUNCIATION GUIDE

Dehaian (deh-HYE-an)

Ina (EE-na)

Kirzan (KUR-zahn)

Neiphiandine (ney-fee-AN-deen)

Niall (nee-AHL)

Nyciena (ny-SEE-en-uh)

Ociras (oh-SHE-rahs)

Reschiata (reh-she-AH-tuh)

Ryaira (ry-AIR-uh)

Sieranchine (see-EHR-an-cheen)

Sylphaen (sil-FAY-en)

Teariad (tee-AR-ee-ad)

Yvaria (ih-VAR-ee-uh)

Zekerian (zeh-KEHR-ee-en)

PROLOGUE

CHLOE

Before we go any farther, I want to make one thing clear: I never intended to run away. I fully intended to go home. I was only taking a vacation.

Even if it didn't end up like that.

You see, I've always been drawn to the ocean. It makes sense, I guess. Growing up in Reidsburg, Kansas, you're about as far from saltwater as you can get without burying yourself underground, and maybe not even then. Figures that something exotic and distant like the sea would attract me.

We all want what we don't have.

But ever since I was a kid, I dreamed of visiting the ocean. Living by the ocean. I'd stare at pictures of the sea in books, memorize the name of every fish I saw, and paint smudges of blue across my preschool art projects and call it the Pacific. My teachers thought it was cute, and my school friends thought I was a bit strange, but I didn't care.

I just knew what I loved.

My parents, though. Oh, they hated it. You'd think someone close to them had drown or been lost at sea or whatever for the anger they showed toward the whole thing. The house was decorated with pictures of deserts, visits to the pool were strictly forbidden – the threat of disease and kids peeing in the water were usually the reasons for that one – and for all our 'vacations', we'd go to Branson, or Oklahoma City or, on one truly impressive trip, a corn museum in Illinois.

A corn museum. Seriously, who visits that?

Well, okay, an agricultural science professor does, I suppose. Which is what my dad is, by the way. But that's beside the point.

They would have rather *died* than let me travel anywhere near the sea. And when my best friend, Baylie, asked if I could come stay with her family at their beach house for two weeks when summer started, Mom and Dad very nearly had a coronary. It wasn't about the fact her gorgeous stepbrother would be there – since, of course, his dad and stepmom were there too and I'd share a room with Baylie anyhow – or even the time I'd be spending away from them. It was just about the ocean. Solely the ocean. And as inexplicably *insane* as anyone could see they were being, my days of arguing, begging, and even bribery got me absolutely nowhere.

But it was the best chance I was going to have, short of hanging around for a year till I graduated – *way* too long to wait, mind you – and then hoping they wouldn't keep me from going to college out west with Baylie, just on the basis it was closer to water.

Because they would. Did I mention they were ridiculous?

So I took matters into my own hands. What else is a girl supposed to do when her best friend offers her a chance to spend two weeks doing something she's always dreamed of? I would had to have been crazy to pass that up.

And I may be many things, but crazy certainly isn't one of them.

So that's how, after packing a small bag, sneaking out my bedroom window, and scaling down a rather loosely bolted drainpipe, I ended up in a car with Baylie and her golden Labrador, Daisy, adamantly *not* running away from home, but instead taking a 'vacation' of my very own.

It turned out so differently than I ever could have imagined.

1

CHLOE

"Well, here we are," Baylie announced, pulling the car to a stop. "What do you think?"

I couldn't take my eyes from the view beyond the car window. For the past few dozen miles, ever since we passed Ventura and the highway curved to meet the sea, I'd been staring. Crystalline water shone under the late afternoon sun, and white-crested waves rolled in to meet the sand. The triangular peaks of sailboats floated across the expanse, while some distance away, a tiny form sped through the air, parasailing beneath the cloudless sky.

It might have seemed silly, but I felt like a kid on their first trip to Disneyland.

"Chloe?" Baylie tried.

"Sorry," I said, managing to pull my gaze away from the window long enough to give her a rueful grin. "It's just…"

I gestured helplessly at the water.

She rolled her eyes. "You're hopeless." Checking her makeup and her long blonde hair in the mirror, she wiped away a bit of smudged mascara beneath her sky-blue eyes and then pushed open the driver's side door. "Just make sure to grab your bag whenever you're done gawking, okay?"

My face flushed in the way it always did when I was embarrassed, splotching my face and every other bit of skin bright pink, and I reached for the door handle, determinedly ignoring her grin. She was well aware I'd always wanted to come here. She'd just known me since we were both four years old, and therefore loved to exercise the best friend's inalienable right to tease.

I climbed out of the red car and then opened the rear door, trying to keep my eyes from straying back to the horizon beyond the beach house. Daisy jumped out, her tail wagging furiously in gratitude for finally being released from the back seat, while Baylie popped open the trunk and retrieved her suitcase, leaving the trunk lid up for me to claim my own bag once I was done with the dog.

On the porch, the screen door slammed. "You made it," Mr. Delaney called, grinning as he jogged down the stairs. Well-built and tall with dark brown hair and equally dark eyes, he strode toward us with an ease that made him seem twenty years younger than his middle-aged status. Taking Baylie's bag, he swung it onto his shoulder and then squeezed her into a lopsided hug. "Perfect timing, too. Diane's just making some snacks."

Baylie made an appreciative noise. Before we'd left Reidsburg, she'd regaled me with stories of Diane's cooking. From the sound of it, even her snacks were bound to be competition for anything the fanciest restaurants back home could've offered.

"Hey, Chloe," he added to me.

"Hi, Mr. Delaney. Thanks for inviting me."

"Of course. More the merrier."

He smiled and motioned for us to follow him toward the house. My eyebrows rose as I registered the size of the place for the first time. Mr. Delaney was the owner of a lucrative software company, and it showed. Despite being only two stories high, his home was more mansion than anything. Mission architecture defined its appearance, though the off-white walls were interrupted by plentiful windows and skylights peppered the tile roof. Positioned on more than two acres of land with a private drive, the sprawling home backed up against bluffs overlooking the sea.

The latter of which was instantly my favorite part, of course.

Smells of bread and spices filled the air as we walked in the front door, adding to the promise of delicious food awaiting us. A ceiling of polished wood beams hung thirty feet high over the foyer, and a stairway to the right of the door led up to the rooms on the second floor. At the end of the hallway, broad windows made up the far wall of the house, through which bright sunlight poured.

A cabinet door slammed, and then a woman popped her

head around the corner at the end of the hall. "Hi there!" she called cheerily. Brushing her palms off on her sides, she hurried toward us and stuck her hand out to me. "I'm Diane – and please do call me Diane, okay? And he's Peter. Like Baylie probably told you, we're pretty informal here. I'm so glad you girls could make it!"

Blinking, I shook her hand. I'd never met her, and only recognized her because of a picture Baylie had shown me on her cell a few days ago, but Diane was even more adorable in person than in her photo. With a brunette bob cut that bounced when she moved and a height of five foot two if she was lucky, she was like an energetic kid, excited by everything she saw.

I could see why Baylie liked her stepbrothers' stepmom so much.

To me, Baylie's family felt complicated, compared to my relatively straightforward status as a single child with one uncle somewhere in Minnesota. Baylie's mom had died of cancer when Baylie was five and her dad had married Peter's ex-wife, Sandra. Thus she had two stepbrothers out here in Santa Lucina, one of whom was three years older than us and the other who was our age. Diane wasn't related to any of them, but had married Peter several years ago. Despite Peter and Sandra's divorce, however, all the adults seemed to have ended up on good terms, which meant Baylie was welcomed like one of Peter's kids by the Delaneys, and her own dad treated her stepbrothers likewise.

It was just confusing for me to keep straight sometimes.

Though, to be fair, my straightforward status wasn't all *that* straightforward either. My one uncle in Minnesota? Yeah, he lived in a psychiatric hospital and last I'd heard, was convinced he was the reincarnation of Napoleon. Or maybe it was Henry the Eighth. But add that to my parents' general insanity, and I had a pretty compelling reason to want to keep every trace of crazy from my life.

"Would you put their bags in their room while I get these ladies settled?" Diane asked her husband.

He nodded and then headed up to the second floor with our bags.

"So neither of you have allergies, right?" Diane continued.

We assured her we didn't.

"Great! So I'm just finishing up a few appetizers for us to have before the cookout tonight – hotdogs good with you? – and then I'm thinking stromboli for dinner tomorrow. Or maybe pizza. You girls like capicola and bresaola?"

Trying to keep up, we assured her we did, though from the look Baylie gave me once Diane's back was turned, I was fairly certain neither of us knew what she meant.

"Excellent! The boys are picking up some at the market as we speak, so the meats should be very fresh. And I'll mix up the rosemary crust from scratch – whole wheat flour too; trust me, you won't go hungry here – so that should complement things nicely."

She kept talking as we walked into the spacious kitchen. A

sunken living room extended off to the left, complete with floor-to-ceiling windows and a fireplace, while a dinner table waited in a glass-walled dining room beyond the kitchen island. A concrete patio with a gazebo and a fire pit took up part of the backyard, while closer to the bluffs overlooking the sea, the wood railing of a stairway led down toward the beach below.

The sound of the front door closing interrupted Diane, and I turned to see Maddox coming down the hall with his younger brother, Noah, several steps behind.

I swallowed. I'd only seen Noah a few times over the years, with the most recent being Christmas when he'd come to visit his mom. I think I'd managed three words. And right now, with his skin tanned golden and his deep green eyes looking amazing beneath the sandy flop of his sun-streaked hair, three words would have been hard to come by.

"Oh hey," Maddox said to us as he came into the room, a paper bag of groceries in his arms. Dark as his brother was light, Maddox took after their father, while Noah had his mother's hair and eyes – though with their height and muscles, they both looked like crosses between surfers and body-builders. Maddox set down the bag. "When'd you all get in?"

"Just a few minutes ago," Baylie said, grinning as Maddox came over and gave her a hug. "You guys went shopping?"

"Eh, well, you know. Gotta help out occasionally." He smiled at me as Noah gave Baylie a hug as well. "Hey Chloe."

"Hey," Noah added to me, twitching his chin in greeting.

"Hi."

Feeling something of an idiot, I looked back to the view beyond the windows, hoping the glare hid any treasonous blushing my face might have decided to do. It was stupid. There were plenty of decent-looking guys that I saw every day back home. Of course, they were local boys and most of them knew me as that girl with the weird parents – which, obviously, wasn't particularly appealing.

And besides, Noah went way beyond decent-looking, straight on to hot.

I could feel my face getting red. Taking a deep breath, I focused on watching the water rolling in.

"So you boys want to get the grill started up?" Diane suggested.

"Sure," Maddox said. From the corner of my eye, I saw him head for the patio door, and Noah followed.

Air escaped me and when I looked back toward the kitchen, I found Baylie watching me curiously.

I pushed a smile onto my face. "Want to get unpacked?"

"Alright," Baylie said.

She headed for the stairs, motioning me to follow.

"You okay?" she asked as we left the kitchen.

"Uh-huh."

She didn't look convinced. And I didn't really want to explain.

"So what one are we in?" I asked as we reached the second floor. I glanced at the doorways lining the hall, trying to cover for the awkward moment.

Baylie led the way to a large bedroom at the end of the long hall. White carpet covered the floor, the same as in the hallway, but the walls here were pale blue. Sheer curtains hung over the window that faced out onto the backyard and the ocean, and two queen-sized beds flanked it. A woven chair stuffed with pillows sat to one side of the room, while a dresser stood nearby, fashionably flaked and vintage-looking paint covering it. Starfish and seahorses were nestled in corners of the ceiling, as were fishermen's nets, while twin skylights let the sun shine down on each of the beds.

"Wow," I said.

"Diane loves decorating almost as much as cooking," Baylie replied with a grin.

I felt like repeating myself, and settled for nodding appreciatively. We headed for our bags, which had been set on the beds. Unzipping my backpack, I hesitated over the contents, and then drew out a sundress. A couple days in a bag hadn't done it any favors, and I glanced toward the rest of my meager wardrobe, trying to recall if I'd stuffed anything else appropriate in there.

My gaze caught on the window. Through the glass, I could see Noah and his brother getting the grill prepared.

Baylie cleared her throat. I flinched.

"Uh-huh," she said.

"What?"

"Nothing."

I glared.

"What? Noah's pretty cute."

There was something weird in her voice. My brow furrowed.

Baylie grimaced. Casting a glance back to the open door, she sighed. "It's just... Look, Noah's great. Really. But lately..." She shook her head. "I don't know. He's not like he used to be. He's... quieter."

I gave her a skeptical look. I couldn't understand how that was a bad thing. At least, not to the degree that she seemed worried about it. "Quieter?"

Appearing uncomfortable, Baylie shrugged. "It's probably nothing."

Her expression belying her words, she went back to pulling clothes from her bag.

I looked to the window. By the grill, Maddox said something, and Noah nodded, his eyes on the horizon. And then he turned, glancing directly at the window behind which I stood.

Alarmed, I stepped back, and then scowled at myself for being so excitable. There wasn't anything odd about what he'd just done. He'd just happened to look up at where I was standing, right when I happened to look down at him.

Which surely was a coincidence.

My goose bumps didn't want to listen. Still scowling, I took the dress and headed away from the window, determined not to let a silly reaction to what had obviously been a fluke moment ruin my evening.

"So I told him 'Only if you take the lobster back too!'"

Everyone laughed, though Noah and Maddox couldn't quite hide an expression like they'd both heard their dad's joke before. Flames crackled in the fire pit in front of us, and the empty plates from dinner still lay to the side of our deck chairs.

"Well, I should get dessert," Diane announced, rising to her feet. Smiling at Peter, she headed for the house.

Silence fell for a moment, and the rush of the tide on the sands filled the quiet. My attention drifted toward the horizon, and the dark water there.

"So you have any summer plans, Chloe?" Peter asked. "Besides this, of course."

I blinked, pulling my gaze back to him. "Not really," I replied, knowing I'd probably be grounded for at least a few weeks when I got home, so there wasn't much point. My parents wouldn't take kindly to me coming out here without their permission. "Just hanging out, I guess."

Peter smiled. "Sounds like fun." He glanced up as Diane came out, a tray of bite-sized cakes in her hands. Bringing them over, she held the tray out to each of us, letting us choose one of the fruit-topped desserts.

"Well, I could go for some volleyball," Peter announced as he finished his cake.

Baylie gulped down her bite of dessert. "But it's dark," she countered, surprised.

"Eh, the court has lights." He gestured toward the sandpit on the far side of the yard. "Besides, it's so dark beyond the court, you can pretend we have spectators watching, like at the Olympics or something."

She laughed as he climbed to his feet. "So who's with me?" Peter asked us.

I couldn't keep the doubtful look off of my face, but the expression just seemed to amuse him.

"Oh, come on," he said, chuckling. "Volleyballs are stored over here."

"I'll join you in a minute," Diane offered, taking up the empty tray and then heading for the house.

Peter nodded. Motioning to the others, he started toward the shed in one corner of the yard. Grinning, Baylie followed him, and Noah shared a humored glance with Maddox as they stood to do the same.

I watched them go, and then turned back to the water. Pushing away from my chair, I headed for the wooden steps leading to the beach.

The stairway ended at the base of the bluffs, and as I left the stairs, my flip-flops sank into the cool sand. A few yards away, the tide slid up the beach and then pulled back, returning to the black water that stretched out until it blended with the sky. Stars glittered like diamonds overhead, their tiny lights pushing past the ambient glow of the city, while far in the distance, clouds gathered, their shapes picked out by the moonlight. For only a heartbeat, a flash of lightning shot down, illuminating the thunderheads and revealing the line of the horizon.

It was beautiful, and everything I'd hoped to see.

My gaze drifting up to the pinprick stars, I walked closer to the water. At the edge of the wet sand, I slipped out of my sandals and then stepped into the gently moving tide.

Tingles spread across my skin as the cool seawater slid around my feet. It felt so *right* here. So perfect and peaceful, yet filled with an energy so vast, I could only begin to perceive it.

And if I could, I'd have spent eternity here just to try.

"Incredible, isn't it?"

Startled, I turned. Noah sat on a fallen rock at the base of the bluffs, his eyes on the horizon like he was reading something in the rolling water.

Frustration hit me, pushing back the edge of the calm that had encompassed me only a moment before. I couldn't figure out how he'd gotten down the steps without me noticing, but I didn't want anyone else here, taking this. Not understanding this. No one ever had, and now that I was standing here, on the edge of the deep, protecting how much it meant to me felt more important than ever.

I shrugged a shoulder. "It's okay," I said, the words so neutral compared to the shivers still running through me that they almost hurt.

He glanced to me, his brow furrowing slightly, as if that hadn't been the answer he'd expected.

"Huh," he replied, a touch coldly. He returned his attention to the ocean.

I bit my lip. My gaze twitched to the horizon and the distant storm there.

"I love it," I admitted.

Looking back, I caught sight of a half-smile flickering across his face. He nodded.

I hesitated and then walked back through the water toward him. He motioned to the large rock, and said nothing as I climbed up next to him.

"Aren't the others going to miss you?" I asked, nodding to the top of the bluffs and the glow from the volleyball court lights.

He shrugged. "They have enough players."

The rush of water became the only sound. My gaze slid around, skirting over the ocean and the sand and trying to find somewhere to be with him only a few inches away. With natural ease, he sat on the rough stone, his feet braced on its side and his elbows propped on his knees. Moonlight traced the edge of his face, silvering his tanned skin and casting him partly into shadow.

I swallowed. He looked incredible. And earlier, he'd been creepy as anything, suddenly glancing up at the bedroom window like he had.

Though that'd just been a coincidence, I tried to remind

myself. I was being ridiculous to let it freak me out.

"So you're Baylie's neighbor," he said into the silence, a question twisting through the statement.

"Yeah."

"Live near her long?"

"Since we were four."

He paused, the timing clicking. "Oh."

The awkward pause stretched.

"Yeah," I filled in. "Her dad moved there before..."

I trailed off. Baylie's mother had died of cancer that next year. It was part of why Baylie and I knew each other so well. She'd spent a lot of time at my house, after school while her dad worked, before he'd married Noah's mom.

Noah nodded.

"You ever been to the ocean before?" he asked after a moment.

I shook my head. "I always wanted to see it, though."

A heartbeat passed as he watched the water. "You could've come with Baylie to visit us sooner."

I glanced at him. He didn't look at me. "It's complicated."

Silence returned. I swallowed, still feeling awkward. It was just the two of us for as far as I could see in either direction, and from the way he was sitting there, he seemed like one of the stones, comfortable with the idea of remaining silently by the seashore for eternity.

Quieter, Baylie had said. I didn't have much to go on for how he'd been before, but now... he was certainly that.

17

I looked down to my legs, absently noting the drying salt from the water glistening faintly on my skin. I probably should just go back up to the house. I wanted to stay, to get as close to the deep water as I dared, but with him here…

"I'm glad you came," Noah said.

I blinked.

"Even if," he acknowledged the words with a shrug, "it's complicated."

I hesitated. "Me too."

He smiled and returned his attention to the water. "I always wondered what it would be like, growing up somewhere else. Somewhere away from the ocean. It's just such a…"

"Force," I filled in when he trailed off.

He looked back. "Yeah," he replied, as though pleasantly surprised.

I could feel heat spreading like wildfire up my neck and I turned my face away, hoping the shadows hid the blush.

"And I can't imagine what that'd be like," he finished. "Not having it nearby."

I hesitated. I didn't know what to tell him. I'd always wanted to come here, and now that I was sitting only a few yards from the water…

It was like a sound you'd heard all your life, but so faintly you'd never noticed it. And now, being so close to the source, almost *immersed* in the amazing, overwhelming source, you suddenly realized what you'd been hearing.

And what you'd been missing.

"Not as nice as this," I whispered.

He looked over at me. I could feel the blush coming back.

"You think everyone feels like that?" he asked.

My mind tossed up a few shining memories of my parents. They'd thrown away every picture of the ocean that I drew in school. They'd ripped pages from books that mentioned the sea. They'd punished me for asking them to paint my room blue.

"No," I answered, certainty hardening my voice more than I intended.

He paused.

"I mean, I'm pretty sure some people don't," I amended, trying not to grimace and hoping he wouldn't ask for more.

He turned to me, and my throat choked from the way his green eyes searched my face. "But you do."

I swallowed. "Yeah."

"Yeah," he echoed. "It seemed like you... I don't know. Like you would."

His brow furrowed and he looked away.

"What?" I asked.

He shook his head. "Nothing."

I watched him, confused, but he just drew a sharp breath and then pushed away from the rock.

"We should get back," he said.

At a loss to figure out what had just happened, I didn't move.

"But," he continued. "My dad does have a boat. We could

19

go out on the water tomorrow, if you want?"

My eyebrows rose. "Uh, *yeah.*"

A smile tugged his lip. "Cool."

Holding out a hand, he waited for me to take it, and then helped me down from the boulder. His fingers lingered on mine for a heartbeat longer than necessary, and the warmth of his skin clung to my hand when he let go.

Still smiling a bit, he headed for the stairs.

A quiver ran through my chest, and I blushed, looking back at the water.

He was strange, a little disconcerting, and definitely quiet in his way, but I was still oddly glad he'd come down here. And not just because my legs felt shaky when he smiled.

It was nice to finally meet someone who saw something I loved in sort of the same way.

"Chloe?" he called from the base of the steps.

"Yep," I replied, his voice snapping me out of my thoughts. Drawing a steadying breath, I followed him to the stairs.

∾ 2 ∾

ZEKE

I'd been out near the Santa Lucina coast for a few hours, ever since leaving Nyciena earlier that morning, and I hadn't found any sign of Ina the entire time. I knew she liked to visit here – the surfers were a favorite of hers to watch – but this time, it seemed she'd tried to be a bit more conniving about sneaking away from home.

Coming to a stop in the water, I grimaced. At this time of day, she was probably joining some tourists for a cookout on the beach or playing around with some new guy she'd spotted on the sands. She had clothes stashed everywhere, did my twin sister, and she loved an excuse to party with humans.

I sighed and checked around briefly. This close to land, nothing below the water was much of a threat, since divers were even simpler to spot after dark and most sharks knew better than to mess with a dehaian. Fishing boats were similarly not a problem, since they were easy to hear from miles away

21

and stank besides. Assured that in my annoyance at Ina, I hadn't missed anything, I flicked my tail in the water and sent myself up to the surface. Air burned on my skin for the heartbeat it took my body to adjust, and I scanned the beach, my eyes compensating easily for the dark.

It was absurd that *I* had to be the responsible one.

My grimace returned. I could have been home right now, making friends with the Deiliora twins. Ina wasn't the only one who enjoyed a party, and damn if those girls weren't sexy as hell. And even if that hadn't worked out, there was also the sirabal championship for all of Yvaria tonight, and I'd wagered three-to-one that the Nycienan Hammerheads would take the title this season.

But instead I was spending the evening hunting for my sister.

Scanning the shore, I didn't see Ina among the tourists and beachgoers on the sand. She might've decided to find some cove from which to watch the storm brewing back out on the water, however, which meant she could be anywhere. Muttering a curse, I dove down again and headed farther up the coastline.

It wasn't even like it was my job to go after her. Dad had any number of people he could have ordered to the task. Hell, he could have sent either of our older brothers as well. But Dad also knew Ina made a game of evading them all where she didn't with me, which meant I got pulled away from my plans and sent to chase her down.

Again.

The water shivered.

I stopped, and then kicked hard up to the surface and scanned the coast.

Everything was the same. There was no earthquake. No explosion. I spun in the water, looking out to sea, but besides the thunderstorm rolling in from a few miles away, nothing at all had changed.

Except quivers still ran through the water around me, like someone had dropped an electrical wire into the ocean.

My brow drew down as I turned back toward the shore. A fire pit burned by a mansion up on top of the bluffs and bright lights shone on a handful of people playing volleyball. Down by the shoreline, a guy sat on a boulder in the shadows, watching a beautiful girl with auburn hair as she dipped her feet into the water.

I paused, studying her. Moonlight glistened on her pale skin and she smiled as her gaze ran across the dark waves. She gave no sign she noticed anything strange about the water. She just radiated calm, as though in the whole world, she was right where she wanted to be.

And her skin was changing.

My alarm returned.

A pale shimmer crept up her legs, the iridescence so faint that only the right angle of the moonlight revealed the alteration. My eyes narrowed, my vision sharpening enough to pick out the hint of scaling inching up from the waterline toward her calves.

And then she turned, seeming startled by a word from the boy, and the iridescence began to swiftly melt away. She hesitated, saying something I couldn't make out, and then she walked back toward him, leaving the waves and crossing the sand to sit by his side.

The quiver in the water vanished.

My brow climbed.

There was no way she'd been causing that.

I scanned the water, but as before, everything was the same. The storm was drifting along the horizon, the night sky overhead was clear, and the people on the bluffs still played their game.

And meanwhile, some dehaian girl had just electrocuted the ocean.

Which was impossible.

I swam a bit closer, my ears beginning to pick out their words over the waves.

"My dad does have a boat," the guy said. "We could go out on the water tomorrow, if you want?"

"Uh, *yeah*," the girl answered, and I could hear the excitement in her voice.

"Cool," the guy replied with his expression twitching toward a smile.

They got up and headed back for the stairs.

I watched her go. She was acting like a human, which made sense. But she'd also let herself start changing in the water, which really didn't. From what that guy had said, he sounded like he lived on land, and if she'd let that go much further, he easily could have seen her change.

Which, really, was just about the most dangerous thing we could do in front of a human.

And then there was whatever she'd been doing to the water, and why.

I glanced back to the waves, frustration hitting me. I wanted to go up there. To find a way to talk to her and figure this out. But as much as I'd like answers, I couldn't just stay here. There was still Ina to consider, and Dad would be furious if I gave up on looking, regardless of the reason.

Above the bluffs, the guy and girl were joining the others, cheering them on as they played their game.

I could do both, I decided. Keep an eye on this girl and look for my sister – assuming Ina didn't just make her way home before I even found her. But whoever this girl was, she had to head back into the ocean eventually, which would give me a chance to ask her what she'd done to the water without risking the humans hearing.

But I'd stay close to the shore, regardless. Something weird was going on; something unlike anything I'd seen. And I wanted to figure it out.

After all, as Ina always said, it wasn't like I didn't have a curious streak.

3

CHLOE

Water lapped at the white hull of the boat and the craft rocked as we climbed on board. The bright morning sun had already heated the deck and the plastic seat was warm beneath me as I sat down. All around us, other boats filled the marina, some of them occupied like ours, and the voices of the passengers carried strangely over the distance.

"Try to have the boat back in by sunset, okay?" Peter called to us from the dock.

I looked back as Noah grinned.

"We will," he replied. Behind the wheel, Maddox just nodded and then turned on the engine.

A shiver ran through the boat. On the dock, Peter undid the moorings with quick motions. Tossing the ropes to Noah, he waited till everything was stored safely and then raised his hand, waving to us as Maddox steered the boat away.

And just like that, we were on the water.

Wind pulled at my hair as we sped beyond the confines of

the marina and the salty spray misted my skin and my swim-suit. Baylie laughed as we bounded over the waves, and I grinned at her, thrilled beyond the ability to speak.

Finally.

That was the only word I could think to describe it. More even than last night, it felt like some sort of switch had been thrown, releasing a pressure that had been building inside over the years without me realizing it. Tension I hadn't known existed just seemed to flow out of me as we left the marina and raced onto the open water. We probably weren't even going as fast as a car in the city, but with the wind rushing around us, I felt like we were flying.

"You like?" Noah called over the noise of the wind.

I could only nod.

A few minutes later, Maddox slowed the boat, killed the engine and then lowered the anchor. At least a mile off, the shore was a mosaic of green mountains and white buildings below. Puffs of clouds drifted over Santa Lucina, but out here, only the barest wisps hovered in the brilliant blue sky. Baylie leaned back on her seat, a smile on her face, while Daisy just eyed the water as though trying to figure out how the demented humans could possibly think this was a good idea.

"So…" Noah started. "Anyone want to go for a swim?"

I smiled. My parents being so psychotic and all, we didn't even have a bathtub in the house, just a stand-up shower the size of a broom closet. I'd never been able to teach myself how to hold my breath underwater, let alone swim.

But that was going to change, starting now.

"Well, um," I began, feeling a bit reckless with excitement. "If you wouldn't mind teaching me?"

His eyebrows climbed. "Uh, no. I mean, sure. I–"

The boat jumped.

"What the hell?" Maddox cried as the rest of us grabbed at the guardrails.

"Did we hit something?" Noah asked, scanning the water.

Maddox shook his head. "I don't–"

The ocean around the boat began to bubble and roil.

Noah swore. "Get us out of here!" he called to Maddox.

His brother didn't need the encouragement. Quickly, he scrambled back toward the driver's seat and turned the key in the ignition.

The engine wouldn't respond.

Shudders shook the boat, while all around, the ocean's surface began to foam like the calm sea had suddenly become a boiling pot on a stove. Waves surged from every direction at once, growing more violent by the second, and on all sides the water darkened, as though a shadow was spreading below us.

"What's happening?" Baylie cried.

No one could answer. As if shoved from beneath, the deck tipped up at a sharp angle and then just as quickly rocked back, wrenching us hard as we fought to hang onto the guardrails. The lurching came again, throwing us forward and back.

My grip broke. The metal rail hit me, knocking the air from my lungs.

And then came the water.

I didn't even have time to scream. Waves closed over me, choking my instinctive gasp and tossing me so hard that, in only a heartbeat, I lost all sense of up and down. Flailing, I tried to reach out and find something, anything, to hang onto as the water pummeled me like it was a prize fighter and I was its punching bag.

Strong hands caught me. Steadied me. Pulled me from the maelstrom into a space of calm. I clutched at them, thinking Noah had managed to find me in the chaos.

Eyes like brilliant sapphires met mine.

"You're okay," a boy said, gripping my shoulders. "You're fine."

I stared at him. In the impossibly black water, I could see nothing but his face and his arms, both pale as though he'd spent his life out of the sun. He seemed only a year or two older than me, and his features were angular, carved like they came from stone, and strangely mesmerizing. In the darkness, his eyes shone like deep blue jewels, simultaneously seeming to reflect light and yet glow from within.

But we were underwater. We should be drowning. And instead, I could hear him as clearly as if we stood in the open air, and the oddest sense of peace was settling over me.

I wondered if I was dying.

His brow furrowed and he ran his gaze over me, as though he couldn't figure out how I was there either. "Who–"

Suddenly, his eyes went wide and his hold on my shoulders

vanished. Other hands grabbed me, snagging my arms, my hands. I struggled, confused and disoriented, as an arm wrapped around my chest and yanked me backward.

My head broke the surface and I coughed, struggling to breathe. Twisting, I saw Noah behind me, holding me while he swam hard for the boat. The white-hulled craft had capsized and Baylie clung to its side, one hand holding Daisy's collar to keep the sodden dog from swimming off. By her side, Maddox was hanging onto the boat as well, though he was stretched out, trying to catch Noah as he swam closer.

But the water had stilled. Waves lapped the upturned hull and pushed us back toward the land.

"Is she alright?" Baylie cried as Maddox grabbed Noah, pulling him nearer to the ship.

Still coughing, I nodded and took Baylie's hand. She tugged me toward the hull and helped me find a grip, while Noah braced me against the side, keeping me from sinking or being forced away by the waves. Air burned on my throat, and my lungs still felt choked. My hair plastered my face, the auburn strands a tangled mess from all the jostling, and with my free hand, I swiped them away.

"Fine," I managed. "What happened?"

"No clue," Noah said. He sounded angry and, as he scanned the ocean around us, he looked it too. A few feet away, his brother's expression was the same.

"There," Maddox called, pointing.

I followed his gesture and spotted a large, white boat racing toward us, the markings of the Coast Guard on its side.

Baylie made a noise of relief. "Oh, thank God."

I seconded the feeling, though as the boat drew closer, I couldn't help but look back at the horizon and the rolling waves. I'd heard people had all kinds of visions before they died – saw their life flash before their eyes or whatever. Shock, adrenaline and God knew what other chemicals could make your mind do all sorts of things when your life was on the line.

Yet that hadn't felt like a bunch of synapses firing because my brain was freaking out from lack of air. That hadn't felt like panic at all.

My hand rubbed at the place on my shoulder where the boy had grabbed me.

That had felt real.

～ 4 ～

ZEKE

The Coast Guard ship cut through the surf and I ducked low beneath the waves, knowing they probably wouldn't see me – or believe what they saw, if they did – but not wanting to take the chance. Overhead, the people still tread water by the hull of their capsized boat, not a single one of them seeming dehaian except for her.

And she only barely.

I stared at her, at a loss to figure out what had just happened. I'd been swimming near the beach to see if Ina had decided to spend the morning on the sand – and planning what I'd say to her if she had; I'd been looking for *hours* – when something had changed in the water. It'd been subtle, and not nearly to the degree of last evening, and for a few minutes, I'd been struggling just to find the source.

And then I'd heard her screaming.

I dropped lower in the water as the white ship drew up beside the capsized boat. By the hull, the blond guy held her close, as if worried she couldn't swim, while on her legs, iridescent threads appeared and then vanished almost as quickly as they formed.

She was fighting it, obviously. With so many humans around, that made sense.

But she'd also been absolutely panicked in the water.

Of course, to be fair, maybe that made sense too. With what I'd seen, I couldn't exactly blame her.

The water had gone mad. I'd swum toward the sound of her screaming beneath the waves to find her being dragged down like she'd been caught in a net. Despite the fact we were barely any distance from the shore, the temperature had dropped to levels ordinarily found in places even deeper than Nyciena, with darkness to match.

And when I'd come close, it'd all started to go away.

I shook my head, baffled. Never in my life had I heard of anything like what I'd just seen, and given my older brother's proclivity for reef camping stories, that was saying something. The girl changed the ocean when she was near it – a statement that on any level should have been impossible. No one affected the water like that. No one could. Boat-sized maelstroms didn't just appear out of a calm sea either, and they didn't bring with them darkness and temperatures normally only found in the true deep.

The Coast Guard pulled her and the others from the water. A few moments passed and then the white ship started back for the shore.

I watched them go. By any definition, this was weird. Truly, truly weird.

And maybe it was time to finally just ask her about it. She was going around like a human. Didn't mean I couldn't too. I'd simply wait for a time when she was away from the others and then talk to her and figure this out. But regardless, I wasn't ready to turn around and go home.

Kicking hard in the water, I followed the boat.

∽ 5 ∾

CHLOE

"What do you mean 'what happened'?" Maddox demanded. "We were just going along and then all hell broke loose! You saw that, right? You couldn't miss it!"

The Coast Guard crewman gave him a warning look, and Maddox made a furious noise, throwing his hands up.

Sitting on the deck with Baylie and Daisy, I watched him storm away, only to be brought up short by another crew-member. Rising to his feet, Noah went to calm his brother down, though one of the Coast Guard intercepted him before he got far. To a person, we were all under watch till they got back to the dock, where hopefully the guys' parents would be waiting.

"They *have* to have seen that," Baylie whispered. "Right?"

I didn't know how to respond. From everything the Coast Guard had said thus far – which wasn't much – they'd simply received a call from a passing ship that a boat had capsized, and they'd rushed out. No one had said anything about churning water or waves that seemed to come from everywhere at once.

Apparently, that'd only been witnessed by us.

And *us* was looking crazier by the minute.

I shifted uncomfortably under the scratchy blanket they'd wrapped me in moments after pulling me onboard. I understood why the others wanted someone to corroborate our story; for insurance purposes alone, it'd be nice to have an official statement saying we hadn't just randomly decided to destroy Peter's boat. But for my part, there was no way what I'd seen *wasn't* impossible, and admitting to it out loud wouldn't help anything.

My gaze slid toward the open water. I pulled it back again, forcing myself to look at the deck and praying I wasn't actually insane.

With her shoulder pressed against mine, I could feel Baylie shivering beneath her blanket, despite the nearly boiling warmth of the summer day.

"You okay?" I asked.

She looked at me, confused.

"You seem frozen."

Her eyebrows climbed. "That water was like ice!" She paused. "You mean you're not cold?"

I hesitated. I hadn't felt cold in the least, and too much more of this blanket and I'd probably melt.

But I couldn't say that.

"Too freaked out, I guess."

She tugged the blanket tighter around her shoulders like it

wasn't the itchiest thing known to God or man. "Guess that makes sense," she allowed.

I swallowed hard, looking at the deck again.

Thankfully, Peter and Diane were indeed standing on the dock when we got in, and as we disembarked from the ship, they seemed more worried about us than anything. Talk of calls to lawyers and the local police commissioner finally allowed us to be packed into the car, rather than kept for further questioning – though the Coast Guard made it clear they wanted to hear from both parties without delay.

Peter smiled and shook hands and handed out his lawyers' business cards, and then bundled us all out of there as quickly as possible.

For which I was incredibly grateful.

"I'm just *so* glad you all are okay," Diane said for the twentieth time as she pulled her sedan up to the house. Ahead, Peter came to a stop as well and then climbed from Maddox's sports car, saying something to his sons that I couldn't hear. Whatever it was, the guys didn't look angry or defensive as they got out after him, though, which I took as a good sign.

"Yeah," Baylie answered for us both.

I managed a smile and then pushed open the door. Baylie followed, still wrapped in the blanket, though she seemed less cold now. Together, we trailed the guys inside.

Diane made a beeline for the kitchen and busied herself with putting a kettle of water on the stovetop, while Maddox disappeared into the next room, still talking in a low voice to his father.

"You alright?" Noah asked, coming up beside me.

I nodded, eyeing the impending tea with nausea twisting my stomach. The whole place was hot enough to have a roaring fire nearby, and they wanted tea? What were they thinking?

It occurred to me that it was strange that, alone of everyone in the room, I'd be this warm.

"Actually," I said to Noah, my throat suddenly tight with the effort of not throwing up. "I... I don't think I'm–"

The world tilted and everything went dark.

I opened my eyes to Diane in front of my face.

And I could see the ceiling behind her.

Jerking away, I tried to turn to the side, only to find Noah there.

A groan escaped me. "What happened?"

"You passed out, honey," Diane said.

My brow furrowed. "Huh?"

Memory started to play back.

I wanted to groan all over again.

Drawing a breath, I moved to sit up and, quickly, Noah put his arm around my shoulders to help. All the embarrassment in the world didn't stop goose bumps from rising on my skin at his touch and I felt a blush race up my neck.

Behind him, Baylie hovered, a worried expression on her face, and as I braced myself on the cold tile floor, she reached out, offering me a glass of water.

"Thanks," I said, taking the glass. Peter, Maddox and Diane were all watching me and I managed a smile, though I kind of wanted to melt through the ground. Trying to ignore my mortification, I focused on taking a drink, while the others straightened and gave each other concerned looks.

I could feel the blush getting worse.

Avoiding their eyes, I set the glass down and then pushed up from the floor. My legs wobbled, my whole body feeling thick and strange, and as I reached my feet, Noah kept his arm on me, steadying me.

I swallowed, quivers running through my body for a whole other reason.

Diane gestured toward the living room. "Why don't you go have a seat in there?" she offered.

Noah led me down the short steps into the sunken room off of the kitchen. The white couch was softer than its sterile appearance gave it credit for, and the breeze coming through the open window carried the smell of the sea.

I closed my eyes as I sat down, breathing in the salty air. The nausea from earlier was gone, and I could only hope the weird feeling in my limbs would fade soon too.

Time slid, and I jerked awake to Noah nudging me.

"Don't sleep," he warned quietly.

I nodded.

"What happened?" he asked, keeping his voice down as he returned to the chair several feet from the couch. In the kitchen, Diane picked up the cordless and headed for the hall, while Maddox and Peter had once again disappeared. Baylie was perched on the barstool by the kitchen island, absently running her bare foot over Daisy's fur and watching me, the same worried look on her face.

I hesitated. I didn't know what to tell him, since I had no idea myself.

"Maybe stress?" I tried with a lopsided shrug. "I mean, what with falling overboard and everything…"

His brow furrowed. "Yeah. Maybe."

Silence returned to the room, broken after a few minutes by the sound of Diane coming back from the hallway.

"Well," she said as she set the phone in its cradle. "It seems things are going to have to be cut short."

"Why?" Baylie asked.

Diane sighed. "I'd hoped perhaps Chloe's parents would approve our doctor taking a look at her, but they're insisting on having their physician back home check her out. They're going to be here soon to pick her up."

I blinked. "Wait, what?"

"Well, honey, I had to call them. You passed out. And I'm really sorry, but since they were on vacation not too far from Santa Lucina anyway, they just want to come get you now."

I'd been wrong. The nausea wasn't gone. Not by a long shot.

And I was so dead.

I swallowed hard. "Ah. Right. Did they, uh, say when they'd be here?"

"They weren't sure. Maybe this evening." Diane smiled. "But hey, we'll have a room set up for them long before then. The more the merrier, eh? You just focus on feeling better."

I nodded as she headed back down the hall.

My gaze went to Baylie. By the kitchen island, she was studying the ground, her expression flabbergasted.

She noticed me watching her, and her eyes twitched between me and Noah.

"What is it?" Noah asked us.

I hesitated. I hadn't really intended to tell anybody, besides Baylie who already knew. It wasn't anyone else's problem. I'd just figured I'd deal with the fallout of my mom and dad being angry when I got home, and enjoy my vacation until then.

So much for that.

"I didn't tell them I was here."

"What?"

I winced at his expression.

"They weren't going to let her come," Baylie explained. "They're, well, a bit crazy and since we were talking about going to the ocean, they sort of…"

"Freaked," I supplied when she trailed off in search of a word to describe the Chernobyl-level meltdown they'd had at the mere suggestion of this trip.

"But," he said, looking confused, "they're on vacation here too."

Baylie scoffed. Noah's brow furrowed.

"My parents would rather die than come anywhere near the coast," I said. "They kind of have a thing about water."

I looked away, grimacing as the pieces clicked. They must have left the second they figured out where the Delaneys lived. And the address wouldn't have been too hard to learn; Baylie's parents probably knew it by heart. All my mom and dad had to do was ask.

"I bet they headed for Santa Lucina the moment they realized you were gone," Baylie said as if reading my mind, and the expression on her face made her opinion of the idea clear.

"You're not serious," Noah replied.

"Oh yeah, I am," Baylie told him.

His brow furrowed as he processed the information. On the white couch, I shifted uncomfortably, feeling like a freak by association.

"Listen, can we get out of here?" I asked. "Maybe go for a walk or something?"

Noah gave Baylie a concerned look.

"I'm fine," I insisted to them both. "I was probably just dehydrated from the saltwater or something. But I'd really like to see more of this place before they get here."

A moment passed.

"Please?"

"The park is pretty nice," Baylie offered, a touch reluctantly.

Noah sighed.

"Great," I said, rising.

My legs wobbled and I froze. Noah stood quickly, grabbing
my elbow to stabilize me.

"Maybe you shouldn't–"

"I'm fine," I told him. Drawing a breath, I straightened and
the shaky feeling in my legs faded. I took a step away from
the couch. "See?"

He didn't look convinced, but he let my arm go.

Baylie hopped down from the chair and I followed her from
the room with Noah a few steps behind. Diane and Peter were
about as reluctant as their son for me to leave the house so
soon after my lovely display in the kitchen, but finally they
agreed. Together with Daisy, the three of us headed out.

As it turned out, the park Baylie mentioned lay at the base
of a gentle slope beyond the thick wall of bushes that surrounded the Delaneys' house, which meant we didn't have
very far to walk at all. I tried not to be disappointed – if I'd
had my way, we'd have been on the other side of town, or
maybe in the next county or state by the time my parents
showed up. But the breeze off the ocean was soothing, and the
grassy area near the beach gave Daisy plenty of space to run.

Sitting down on a bench close to the sandy shoreline, I
attempted not to fidget too uncomfortably as Noah joined me.
The smoothie I'd purchased from one of the carts along the

promenade sweated in my hand and slowly froze my fingers. Several yards away, Baylie kept an eye on Daisy, and tossed her a branch we'd picked up as we walked along.

"So," Noah began.

I watched him from the corner of my eye.

"Pretty crazy, that stuff on the boat," he continued.

I looked down, embarrassed. "Thank you for... you know."

He shrugged. "No problem."

Daisy ran toward a group of birds beneath a palm tree a hundred yards away. Yelling at her, Baylie followed.

"So you really didn't tell anyone you were coming here?"

I grimaced, looking away.

"Sorry," he said. "I just... that's pretty crazy too."

"It's normal," I replied.

My tone sounded defensive, and my response was too fast, and I could tell he heard it.

"Going to visit the ocean," I explained, trying to keep my voice calm. "It's normal to just take a vacation. They're the ones who're crazy."

He paused. "They really hate *water*? Like, that's why they didn't want you to come?"

I nodded.

He thought for a moment. "They're the ones who don't feel the same way you do about the ocean," he said, as though filling in a blank. "That's who you were thinking of last night."

I hesitated and then nodded again.

His brow shrugged in amazement.

I looked back at the water. Waves rolled toward the shore from a horizon that was nothing but shades of beautiful blue.

"They're missing out on so much," I whispered, watching the tide.

I realized I'd spoken the thought aloud, and I glanced to him hesitantly.

He had that look in his eyes again. Like he understood.

"Yeah," he agreed.

I drew a breath, some of the tension leaking out of me.

"So... what happened?" he asked carefully. "To make them like that, I mean. Did somebody in your family drown or something?"

"No. I don't know what their deal is." I paused, working to adopt a lighter tone. "I mean, I *do* have an uncle who thinks he's related to the seahorses at the Mall of America aquarium. But he also thinks he's Napoleon, so that's probably not it."

Noah blinked. I watched him, hoping he'd find it funny and not just wonder if the insanity was genetic.

"You're joking," he said.

I shook my head.

He paused.

"They're just nuts," I said more seriously. "Protective, but on steroids. They wouldn't let me take P.E. at school, do sports, any of it. But water... that's their big thing." I shrugged. "I don't know why."

He was silent for a moment. "Must've been hard growing

up with them."

I tried not to grimace. I hadn't intended to sound like a victim. They were probably certifiable, it was true. If it hadn't been for Baylie and her family continually giving me a place where I could hide from the crazy, God knew what I would've ended up like. But that didn't mean I wanted pity.

Especially not his.

"They're nuts," I acknowledged. "But you have to keep it in perspective. I mean, I'm not. Baylie's not. I'm fairly certain you and most of the rest of the world aren't..."

I gave him a hopeful grin.

Noah hesitated, his lip twitching. "Last time I checked. I'm not sure about the rest of the world, though."

My grin broadened. "Regardless, it's still perspective."

He gave a slow nod, and then turned back to the water. A heartbeat passed.

"You're amazing, you know," he said quietly.

My grin faltered, and a blush raced up my neck. I dropped my gaze to the smoothie melting in my hand. "I-I'm not–"

He looked back to me. "Really."

I swallowed. My face could probably have masqueraded as a stoplight for how red it felt. "Thanks," I managed, returning my gaze to the smoothie. "You, um... you too."

He paused.

"Hey," Baylie called, jogging up to us. "You guys want to head toward the pier? Daisy's done about all the damage she can to the heart rates of the bird population here."

"Yeah, sure," Noah said, and to my ears, his voice sounded a bit tight.

Though it might have just been my imagination.

He took a breath and pushed to his feet. I followed, glancing back to see Daisy racing off after another seagull that had foolishly landed in a hundred-yard proximity.

The boy from the ocean stood at the edge of the park.

I froze. In the early afternoon light, his black hair glistened. Slender, but in the way a steel cable was slender, he was paused with one hand resting on the trunk of a palm tree.

And his eyes were locked right on me.

"Chloe?" Noah said.

Gasping, I glanced to him and Baylie. "Do you see—"

The boy was gone when I looked back.

My gaze darted around the park, landing on tourists and volleyball players and people in rollerblades and not finding him anywhere.

But I'd seen him. I had.

Or else I'd been *really* hasty in telling Noah I wasn't insane.

"Chloe?" Noah tried again. "What is it?"

My heart pounding, I looked back at him. "Sorry, I, um… nothing. Just thought I saw someone."

I plastered a grin on my face, though I could feel how tense it was, and I was fairly certain he could see it too.

"Okay," he allowed. He gave Baylie a small glance, and then continued to me, "The pier sound alright to you?"

"Sure."

The grin was going to crack. I started walking, my gaze twitching to the place where the boy had been standing.

No one was there.

Noah's cell phone buzzed.

I nearly jumped out of my skin.

Noah stared at me as I turned back. "Are you okay?" he pressed.

Still clinging to my swiftly fracturing grin, I nodded.

His phone buzzed again. He didn't take his eyes off me as he pulled it from his pocket.

"Yeah?" he answered. A moment passed, and when he spoke again, disbelief filled his voice. "Already?"

My heart sank.

"Okay," he sighed. "Be there soon."

He returned the phone to his pocket.

"They're here," I said.

"Just pulled up."

I looked away.

"I'm sorry, Chloe," Baylie said.

I nodded.

Noah glanced to Baylie. Reluctantly, they started back toward the house, bringing Daisy in tow. Closing my eyes, I took a breath and then followed.

Mom and Dad's green sedan was parked out front when we arrived.

I paused at the edge of the driveway, half-expecting them

48

to be in their vehicle ready to go. But nothing moved behind the smoked windows and after a moment, I drew a steadying breath, making myself head inside.

The silence was worse than anything, like the calm before the storm that tears your house down. By the door, my backpack was already waiting. As I walked to the kitchen, I found Mom and Dad sitting on barstools next to the island, stiff as sculptures with glasses of ice tea untouched beside them. By the counter, Diane and Peter looked past me to Noah and Baylie, and I could see the displeasure with them both beneath their polite expressions.

"Well, thank you for your hospitality," my dad said, his voice tight as he rose to his feet. "But we'd better be going."

Mom gave them a pinched smile as she followed my dad across the room. "Come on," she told me as she walked past.

I looked between everyone. "They…" I started, and then trailed off. I didn't even know what my parents had said to the Delaneys.

"Chloe," Dad called.

"Whatever they told you," I pressed on, "it's not Noah or Baylie's fault."

Glancing to Noah, I tried for a smile, and then trailed my parents to the door. Hefting my backpack, Dad put it in my arms and then nodded toward the car.

I went. Reaching their sedan, I swung my bag onto the seat and then reluctantly climbed in. Dad shut the door behind me and then joined my mom in the front. The sedan quivered as he turned it on, and gravity pushed me back as he accelerated away. Ignoring the speed, my mother drew a tight breath as she tucked a lock of her wavy brown hair behind her ear.

And neither of them said a word.

I sighed, looking back toward the horizon through the smoked windows. Sunlight glistened on the waves and seagulls flew in lazy arcs through the sky. Boats cut myriad lines through the blue expanse, and behind several of them, bright-colored water-skiers skimmed along. Even through the haze of the darkened windows, it was still a beautiful day.

And I'd be back to see more of them.

Clinging to the thought, I kept watching the water till the car turned again and the ocean view was obscured by bushes and trees. Following a twisting path through town, Dad steered the car toward the state highway, his every motion tense and angry.

And then he turned north.

My brow furrowed.

Continuing on, he traced the highway for a few miles and then took an exit to another state road leading even more sharply north.

I turned around, looking through the rear window.

Surely not.

I restrained an incredulous scoff. They weren't going back the way Baylie and I came. And the only reason I could think of was that the main road ran along the water and, owing to the curve of the coastline, these roads led directly away from it.

Wow. Just… wow.

"What were you *thinking*, Chloe?" my mother hissed, her voice barely audible over the road noise.

I glanced to her. She twisted around in her seat, pinning me with a furious glare.

"We heard about your little boat trip," she told me.

"I'm fine."

She scoffed, the sound nearly what I'd kept myself from making a few moments before.

But that's family for you. Get angry the same way.

"No thanks to your own foolishness," she retorted. "You're just lucky the Coast Guard pulled you out when they did."

I turned to the window.

"You look at me when I'm talking to you, young lady."

I ignored her.

"Chloe Marie Kowalski!"

"Listen to your mother, Chloe," Dad ordered. "You have no idea how lucky you are. There are bacteria in seawater. Dangerous animals too. Killer sharks. Sting rays–"

I wasn't able to hold back the scoff this time.

"You could have died!" Mom snapped.

I gave her an incredulous look.

Her glare deepened. "It's dangerous out there, Chloe. There are diseases, and rabid animals, and crazy people. The world isn't one big playground for you to go tromping around in, young lady, and I just hope you learn that before it hurts you."

I turned away with a groan.

"You're grounded," she said.

"Figured."

"Till Christmas."

My eyebrows climbed as I looked back to her. "*Huh?*"

"You heard me."

"You are *not* serious."

"Oh, yes I am. Your father and I discussed this on the two-day drive you made us take to get out here."

"I didn't *make* you–"

"We told you no about this trip, and you came anyway. What were we supposed to do?"

"Let me! It was just a short–"

"No. It was you being obstinate, and that ends now. We know what's best, Chloe. You need to learn to obey us on these things."

I glared at her, my skin crawling at the word. Obey. They loved that one.

"Also," Dad added. "We're moving."

My glare faltered as my jaw dropped. "Wait... *what?*"

"Moving," my mom repeated. "Baylie has obviously been a bad influence on you. Her whole family, for that matter. We think it would be better if we didn't live next to them any longer."

"No," I protested. "No, I am *not*–"

52

"Yes, you are. We've already spoken with a realtor on the phone, and we have appointments to see houses in Salina when we get back."

"You're leaving *town?*"

"*We* are," Mom corrected. "I don't know what you expected here, Chloe. You ran away from *home*, thanks in no small part to that girl. There are consequences to that kind of behavior."

I couldn't believe this. It was like some bizarre nightmare where people told you things more horrible than you could have imagined in your waking hours, all while acting as though those things were somehow completely acceptable to say.

"You can't do this."

They didn't respond. Mom just turned around to face the front and Dad kept driving like nothing had happened.

I stared. They didn't care. They thought they were right, and that was all there was to it. Yet surely that couldn't be all, because there was no *way* they'd move simply because I'd–

But of course they would, I realized. Of *course* they would. They were insane. Utterly, completely, and all otherwise insane.

And now they were going to take me away from one of the only friends I had in the world.

I looked back out the window, my mind reeling as I tried to figure out what I was going to do now.

6

ZEKE

From the bushes by the edge of the yard, I watched as a man and woman loaded the girl into a car and then sped away like they were fleeing a tidal wave. Whipping around the turn of the drive, they barely slowed as they reached the main road, and in only a few heartbeats, they were gone.

And on my list of bizarre things in the past day, that ranked pretty high.

Not that it mattered.

I muttered a curse. Weirdness upon weirdness, and now she was gone. I didn't know how to follow or where to search for her next, either. I'd managed to find her here only because it seemed a safe bet the humans would return to the place they'd been the day before, and because she'd gone on a walk with that blond guy and another girl in the park. She'd never left their company though, meaning I'd had no chance to ask her what was going on.

I looked to the house, but the humans hadn't come back

outside. And it wasn't like it'd do any good to ask them about her. She'd been hiding what she was from them, and I was a stranger. I didn't even know the girl's name.

There was no way they'd volunteer her whereabouts or have answers about what happened today.

Frowning, I left the bushes and walked back the way I'd come. I should have just interrupted her. Gone over and asked to speak to her privately or something. But when she'd spotted me on the far side of the park, fear had come into her eyes, as if the sheer sight of me terrified her. It'd gotten better after I moved to another location where I couldn't be spotted as easily, but still, she'd looked really shaken.

And as with everything else, that made *no* sense, and left me with even more questions than before.

I scowled. There was nothing for it. Mystery or not, she was gone.

And I'd put off looking for Ina long enough.

I headed into the park. People shot past me, wheels on their feet that it took me a minute to remember the name for, and others walked along, being led on ropes by dogs. The sun was bright overhead, and hot too, and it cooked against the t-shirt and shorts I'd retrieved from my stash of supplies farther up the coast.

"Hey!"

I turned to see Ina jogging toward me. Her long, black ponytail bobbed and flashed in the sunlight and she wore denim shorts below a scale-formed imitation of a bikini top.

"Be right back!" she called over her shoulder to a group of guys standing by a small cluster of trees.

"Where the hell have you been?" I demanded as she came closer.

"Whoa, take it easy," she laughed. "Dad have you out looking for me?"

"Since yesterday."

She winced. "Eesh."

"Ina…"

"What? Look, I'm sorry, okay? It's just… Egan and I had a fight and–"

I groaned. Her boyfriend again. The latest one, in any case. I should have known.

"I needed some time away," she protested. "And honestly, I don't get the big deal. I'm a big girl. I can take care of myself."

Grimacing, I looked to the coast. She and I both knew that where Dad was concerned, that wasn't the point.

She shifted around uncomfortably. "Did you at least get to do anything fun while you were out looking for me?" she asked, clearly trying for a peace offering. "Meet some surfer girls or…"

She trailed off hopefully.

I gave her a dry look. "Not exactly."

Her eyebrow rose. My mouth tightened.

"Were you out oceanwise last night? Maybe two hours after sunset?"

She nodded. "Luke and I both were." She glanced to one of the muscle-bound surfers standing near the trees and then grinned at me. "For a human, he's pretty decent in the water."

I ignored the comment. I knew she was smart enough not to lose control and take things too far with a human, no matter how much Dad worried she would. "You feel anything strange happen around that time?"

Her brow furrowed. "You know, now that you mention it, there was something that felt kind of odd. It went away pretty quick though."

"I found what it was."

She waited.

"There was a girl. Dehaian, but staying with a bunch of humans in that white mansion by the park. I saw her on the beach last night and when she touched her feet to the water…"

Ina looked at me like I was joking. "No way."

"Seriously."

"It had to be a coincidence."

"It stopped the minute she went back to shore."

Ina's brow rose.

"There's something weird about this girl. You hear someone screaming earlier today? Dehaian, I mean."

She shook her head. "We were in a surf shop downtown."

"The waves attacked her, Ina. I was there. I saw it. The latter part, at least. It was creepy as hell, and when I came closer, it just went away."

"She see you?"

"Yeah. She seems afraid of me, though. She spotted me just a little bit ago and looked terrified."

"And you're sure–" Ina glanced back at the guys under the tree and lowered her voice, "you're sure she's dehaian?"

I nodded.

"Huh." She thought for a second. "You want me to try talking to her? Maybe she's just scared of guys or something."

"A man and woman just came to the house where she'd been staying and took her away in a car."

"A car."

I nodded again.

"She was staying in a house and they took her away in a car," Ina repeated.

"Yep."

"Okay, yeah, that is weird. I mean, weirder. Or..." She shook her head.

Silence fell between us for a moment.

"You going to head home now?" she asked me.

I hesitated.

A grin twitched her lip. "You want to figure this out, don't you?"

"The girl electrocuted the ocean by stepping into it, Ina."

Her grin broadened. "So what are you going to do?"

"What can I do? She's gone, and from the way those people drove out of here, I doubt they're thinking of coming back."

"You don't know that."

I looked away. This was true.

"Hang around a few days," Ina suggested. "See if she shows up somewhere nearby. If she's really dehaian, it's not like she'll be able to stay out of the ocean forever, and if she does stuff like that every time she's in the water…"

I grimaced.

"Oh, come on," she teased, "you know you want to."

I didn't answer.

"Zeke…"

I sighed. "A few days. And what're you going to do?"

She grinned.

"Ina…"

"Okay, *fine*. I'll go home. Just let me say goodbye to Luke."

I glared as her expression took on an impish tinge.

"I'll be back in Nyciena by morning," she assured me, still grinning.

"*Tomorrow* morning?"

"Yes, tomorrow morning."

I shook my head, but I couldn't stop my mouth from twitching as well.

"So this girl…" Ina prompted. "She cute?"

I made an exasperated noise. This wasn't about that. The girl electrocuted the ocean. Yes, she was attractive. She was damn near gorgeous when she wasn't staring at me like I was a two-headed shark. But she was also a total unknown and, again, she *electrocuted* the *ocean*. I needed to find answers to that before I let myself get caught up in anything else.

"Oh, come on!" Ina protested at my silence. "Since when are you so uptight?"

My grimace returned. "Yes, she's cute," I admitted. "Cream-scaled, by the look of it. Reddish hair. Green eyes."

"Sexy."

"You're incorrigible."

"Damn straight."

I chuckled, shaking my head again.

She smiled and took my hand. "Take care of yourself and I'll see you when you get home, okay?"

"Okay."

She gave my hand a squeeze and then turned, jogging back to the surfers. Muscle-bound Luke slid an arm around her the moment she came close, and tossed me a warning look for good measure.

I tried not to scoff. He really had no idea how much trouble he'd be in if he tried to push things with Ina. And that was just from her.

Giving them a wide berth, I walked back toward the water. Hanging around a few days wouldn't be hard. I just hoped the girl would come back soon, because Ina was right.

I'd hate to leave with this still a mystery.

❀ 7 ❀

CHLOE

Dad drove on long after the sun had set, tracing a winding path through the mountains and the Mojave desert and then onto the interstate through Nevada. Las Vegas swept by, radioactive in the darkness, and sometime after that came Utah.

And beyond brief pauses for gas, he didn't stop.

Mom hadn't said a word to me since we left Santa Lucina, and Dad only occasionally looked back at me in the rearview mirror. I'd taken to ignoring them both, and eventually just pillowed my head on my bag and stared out the window. The white-noise drone of the tires lulled me, pulling my eyes closed as the hours crept along, until I finally drifted off to sleep.

The first thing I saw was water.

I wanted to flail, to scream as I plummeted into it, but the ocean just closed over my head, swallowing the sky and the clouds. Water engulfed me as an invisible force propelled me down, driving me onward till the sea surrounded me completely.

And then it slowed. Stopped. Spreading my arms, I hovered in the water, at a loss to know how deep I'd fallen. The current wrapped around me then, and my skin tingled as it carried me gently through the endless blue twilight.

But I wasn't frightened anymore.

I paused, struck by the realization. The fear I'd felt at first hitting the water had vanished, and now I just knew I was safe. Even under the water, even without any air, I wasn't in any danger at all.

Because I belonged there.

Confusion filled me at the thought, which was impossible and yet true.

I was where I was supposed to be.

On the heels of that understanding came hurt. An ache in my chest that didn't seem to want to go away. I was where I was supposed to be, yet I wasn't. I was leaving, even as I floated in the infinite deep, because this wasn't reality.

This was just a dream.

My eyes opened. The world was dark. The only light came from the pale orange-red glow of the dash and the twin beams of the headlights on the empty stretch of road. Dad was still driving, while in the passenger seat, Mom slept with her head pillowed on her curled arm.

Air escaped me. Tears stung my eyes and in my chest, I could still feel an ache like someone had stabbed me in my sleep, and everything I had was bleeding out through the wound. My body was tense, and as I twisted in the seat to look out the rear window, I felt like invisible threads extended from my skin, over the mountains all the way to the sea, each of them growing thinner and weaker the farther Dad drove.

And if they snapped, I wasn't sure what I'd do.

Swallowing, I turned back to the front, and my hands wrapped around my elbows to hug my middle. It was ridiculous, getting so upset over a dream. But it had felt so real, and the sense of the water around me had seemed so right...

So beautifully, wonderfully *right*...

In my chest, the ache grew worse and I bit my lip, trying to keep myself together. I needed to go back. Not because my parents were moving, or because I'd always wanted to visit the ocean. But because I *had* to.

The alternative made me feel like screaming.

I looked at Dad, willing him to stop. He and Mom seemed committed to driving back to Reidsburg at top speed, and given the time on the dashboard clock, they didn't intend to stop at all.

But I couldn't handle that. I needed to leave.

And Dad just kept driving.

Minutes trickled by, while the miles stretched like rubber bands on the verge of breaking. I wanted to crawl out of my skin.

And then the lights of a city came into view. Barely holding back a gasp, I glanced to Dad again.

Reaching over, he nudged Mom. With a sharp breath, she woke, and then a grimace twisted her face and she gave an uncomfortable groan.

"Drive?" he asked, his voice strangely tight.

Mom swallowed, and then she shook her head. "Not doing well," she murmured. "Medicine wearing off. I… I can watch."

My brow furrowed, but he just nodded and kept driving while Mom leaned back against the window again. The highway continued on through the sleeping town, and our car followed it.

I wanted to cry.

And then, at the final exit, he steered the car onto the off-ramp.

Relief hit me and I gasped with the force of it. Turning at a lonely stoplight at the end of the exit ramp, he sent the sedan toward a tiny building nearly lost in the darkness. A red vacancy sign glowed beneath the dim and flickering letters of the word 'Motel', the only indication of the place's identity. By the front door, he pulled to a stop and then climbed out.

I looked at Mom and then at the darkness around us. I could run. Just make a break for it right now. I knew she wasn't feeling well, and honestly, taking advantage of that was probably a crappy thing to do to my own mother. But I really, *really* needed to leave.

Dad returned, a room key in his hand. Getting back in, he glanced to Mom and then started the car again. By the last door in the row of narrow, brown doors, he pulled over. Only three other cars shared the dark parking lot with us, and above the sidewalk running alongside the motel, half of the rusting light fixtures were missing bulbs.

I couldn't believe they were stopping here.

Without bothering to get out any bags, Dad left the car and headed for the room, while Mom just took a deep breath and then shoved the door open. Bracing herself on the car roof, she paused and looked back at me.

"Come on," she ordered.

I took my backpack and got out. Waving a hand at the door, she waited for me to go ahead of her, never taking her eyes off me.

Fighting back a grimace, I went.

The room was dank, that was the first impression. And beyond that, it didn't get much better. Thin comforters in faded Southwestern patterns covered the two queen-sized beds, and a boxy television sat on a wooden table so chipped and scratched, it looked a heartbeat from collapsing into matchsticks. A salmon-colored lamp stood on the nightstand between the two beds, along with an alarm clock blinking the wrong time. At the far end of the room, a mirror hung over the sink, reflecting the hideous space back at us, while a door waited beside it, giving access to what I could only assume was the bathroom.

Mom shut the door behind me, and then walked to the bed and sat down with a sound somewhere between a groan and a sigh. Dad emerged from the bathroom, not looking much better than her. Tiredly, he took the chair from the corner and dragged it over by the door.

"You sure?" he asked Mom.

She nodded, pushing away from the bed and crossing to the chair, where she sat down. Dad scrubbed his hand across his face and then started toward the bed, when he caught sight of me staring at them both.

He hesitated. "There might be thieves," he told me, a note of discomfort in his voice.

I rolled my eyes. They'd never been this paranoid when we'd stayed at any of the spots they chose for vacations. But now, Mom was squarely between me and the door, and both she and Dad were watching me like hawks.

Though given how much I wanted to race out the door right then…

But that wasn't the point. They were standing *watch* on me, for goodness sake, and claiming it was because there might be thieves.

Would it have killed them to just tell the truth?

"Why are we here?" I asked, not bothering to keep the disgust from my voice.

"Because it's cheap and we're not staying long," Dad responded, his tone harder. Leaving Mom by the door, he took my backpack from me and set it on the bed farthest from the exit. "So get some sleep. We're leaving at sunrise."

He regarded me, waiting. I crossed the room and snagged my backpack from the bed. Eyeing them, I walked into the bathroom.

I could hear them begin talking the moment I closed the

door, though their voices were too low for me to make out the words. But they sounded agitated.

A scowl twisted my face. Still holding my bag, I leaned back against the door.

How was I going to get out of here?

I closed my eyes. My chest ached with my distance from where I knew I had to be, and even without any windows to help me get my bearings, I felt like I could lift my hand to point and know I was aiming directly at the closest part of the ocean.

Which was nuts.

But no more so than the rest of this.

I let out a breath and looked down. If I didn't put on my pajamas, they'd know I meant to leave as soon as possible – though, honestly, they were probably aware of that anyway. They *were* watching the door.

Rolling my head to the side, I looked in the direction of the motel room. Did they know about this? About how I was feeling? Was that why they were acting even more freakish than usual?

The ache grew. But if they knew, they'd understand. They'd get why I needed to go back. They'd support me.

Unless there *was* something truly horrible out there...

I pushed the thought away. I knew what I'd felt when I'd fallen off the boat. What I'd felt in that dream. I'd been safe. Under the water... but safe.

And now I just needed to go back.

I glanced down at the bag again. Pajamas would slow me down. Mean I had to change clothes before I left.

But again, I couldn't give them more of a tip-off to my plans than they already had.

Feeling sick, I drew out my pajamas. With a deep breath to steady me, I forced myself to get dressed for bed.

They were watching the bathroom when I came back out.

"Goodnight," I told them flatly.

They echoed the word, their voices cautious. Ignoring them, I pulled back the thin comforter and the vaguely humid-feeling sheets, and then climbed beneath them.

Dad got into the other bed. Leaning over, he switched off the bedside lamp.

Darkness swallowed the room. By the door, Mom shifted around on the chair, resulting in a faint metallic squeak.

And then everything was still.

Loss and distance pressing on my chest till it hurt to breathe, I closed my eyes and tried not to sob.

"You think she's... you know?"

The whisper cut through the water surrounding me, pulling me away from the deep and the calm. My brow furrowed as I tried to hang onto the dream.

It didn't do any good. The ocean faded. The cloying sheets of the motel bed returned.

"I'm not sure," Dad replied, his voice quiet.

Mom made a worried noise. "We need to get going."

"What about you? Are you any better?"

"No." Annoyance mixed with the worry in her tone. "It was too long." She paused. "You?"

Dad didn't answer.

"Bill?" she pressed.

"I'm okay." The bed rustled as he rose, and then the springs gave a sharp squeak. It sounded like he'd sat back down.

"No, you're not," Mom countered.

He made a shushing noise. I kept my eyes closed and focused on making my breathing as even as possible.

"I can still drive," he insisted quietly. "Linda, I mean it. I'll get us home."

Mom didn't say anything. A moment passed. The front door opened and then closed.

She sighed and got up, the chair giving the same metallic complaints as she moved.

"Chloe?" she called.

I opened my eyes. Standing by the foot of the bed, she was watching me.

She looked pale. Drained. And she was studying my face like she was searching for something.

"What?" I asked.

"Are you doing okay?" She almost sounded concerned.

"Fine."

She paused. "We just want what's best for you, sweetheart."

I didn't say anything.

For a heartbeat longer, she hesitated, and then she returned to her chair.

My brow furrowed. "*You* alright?"

"I'm fine. Get dressed. We're leaving."

She closed her eyes and drew a breath as though she was fighting off nausea.

"Mom?"

"You heard me."

I paused. Not taking my eyes from her, I reached into my bag and got out my jeans. Beneath the covers, I pulled them on and then grabbed my shirt, doing the same.

She exhaled sharply.

"Mom, you don't seem–"

Rising to her feet, she bolted toward the bathroom. I stared after her, and then winced at the sound of retching coming past the door. Feeling vaguely sick myself, I turned my face to the rest of the motel room.

The empty motel room.

My hands grabbed my backpack before I'd even finished registering the thought, and my legs scrambled to escape the blankets. My feet jammed themselves into my shoes, and in only a second, I was at the front door.

And then my conscience caught me. Mom was sick. *Really* sick, for no reason I could see. Something could be seriously wrong with her.

I trembled, the dream still clinging to me and the feeling

of threads stretching to the ocean pulling at my skin like fishhooks.

If I didn't go now, I'd probably never have another chance. They'd probably never give me one.

It was now or never.

I twitched aside the curtain and peeked out the window.

Dad was by the car. Leaning on the car. He looked nearly as sick as Mom.

I yanked open the door and took off running.

"Chloe!" he shouted.

My shoes pounded on the concrete as I dashed across the parking lot. The motel office flashed past, and then came the street, and I cast a quick look over my shoulder, checking his distance from me.

He was in the car. He was coming.

The empty road was behind me in a moment, delivering me into the abandoned lot across from the motel. Weeds and broken asphalt filled the space, and the pale light of the coming sunrise touched everything with hazy pink. A chain-link fence bordered the property, with scrub-grass fields beyond. Fighting for more speed, I ran for them both.

Metal scraped as his sedan jumped the curb and bounded onto the lot behind me.

Gasping, I ducked low and darted through a gap in the fence.

Tires screeched and I heard a car door slam. I kept running. Hidden holes threatened to trip my feet, and the grass was slippery with morning dew, soaking my tennis shoes. But there were houses ahead, squat and mostly identical, and houses meant roads and hidden corners and places he'd have a harder time reaching me.

I heard the chain links rattle. I struggled to run faster.

"Chloe, you get back here this minute!"

Like that was going to happen.

I reached the backyard fence of the nearest house. Grabbing the top, I hoisted myself over and dropped to the wet grass.

"Chloe, *please*!"

One hand bracing me on the fence, I looked back. He was still running, though much more slowly than I'd expected. Pain twisted his face and his feet stumbled with every few steps.

Worry flickered through me, but there wasn't any time.

He'd just force me to come back with him.

And the mere thought of that made it hard to breathe.

Pushing off the fence, I ran for the gap between the house and its neighbor. A simple latch secured the gate, letting me out almost immediately, and then I was at the next street. Little gray houses lined the road, without much more than flower pots or the occasional forgotten toy to differentiate them. The street turned ahead of me, leading farther into town, and I dashed along it.

Exhilaration pounded through me. I was going to make it. I'd find a bus station, use the debit card in my bag to get a ticket, and then I'd be on the road to the ocean.

Even if this was all *completely* insane.

The thought was distracting and I shook my head, driving it away. I'd felt better when I was on the water. Better than I felt now and better than I'd ever felt in my life. I remembered that. I *knew* that. I just needed to find my way back to the ocean by Santa Lucina, and then I'd figure everything else out.

Even if I had no idea *why* I had to be there or, at the moment, where I was actually going.

My feet faltered and I stumbled, barely stopping myself from falling. Regaining my balance, I kept running, though slower than before. Street signs passed, each of them useless since I had no idea where I was headed, and the neighborhood felt like it would never end.

I couldn't believe I was doing this. Running away in a city whose name I didn't even know, for reasons that made no logical sense, all in the hope of getting back across hundreds of miles to where I'd been yesterday.

But I *had* to. The idea of doing anything else just set my heart racing with panic again.

The neighborhood opened out onto a city street with shops that were still closed from the night before. But on the corner, a bus was paused, its doors open for the handful of people waiting to climb onboard.

I glanced around, not seeing my dad or his car anywhere, and then ran for the bus stop. The driver gave me a funny look as I clambered inside and fumbled the requisite cash from my bag, but I just smiled, hoping he wouldn't ask me anything.

At a seat several rows from the front, I sat down. Reaching back into my bag, I pulled out my phone. There was a good chance my parents would call the cops. I couldn't see why they wouldn't. But maybe, if I was fast, I could find the main bus station and make it out of town before they sent the police to find me.

Tapping the screen, I brought up the web browser and then typed in a search.

A smile tugged my lip as the results appeared. The local, intercity bus station wasn't far from here. And there was a bus departing westward soon.

I looked to the road again, checking the street signs that had suddenly become so much less useless than before. Minutes passed until the intersection I needed came into view, and quickly, I yanked the cord to request the driver to stop.

It felt like his gaze tracked me the whole way off the bus.

The station was a tiny brick building only a single story high. A garbage bin blocked one of the doors, and the other bore a handwritten sign demanding that I close it tightly for the sake of the air conditioning. Eyeing the place dubiously, I walked inside.

There weren't any cops. Only a few people occupied the cramped waiting room. I crossed the tile floor to the ticket counter and bought a one-way trip to Santa Lucina, knowing that even if the debit card transaction *would* tell my parents where I was going, it wasn't like they weren't going to be able to predict that anyway. Clutching my ticket, I headed for a seat, and then froze as the intercom buzzed, announcing boarding for the bus.

A thrill ran through me. This could actually work. It was psychotic, and in no way made any sense whatsoever... but it could work.

Feeling ridiculous, but somehow unable to find it in myself to care, I followed the other passengers out the door.

After we passed the desert, I felt better, and by the time the bus pulled into the station, almost every trace of the panic that'd gripped me the day before had gone. The insistent drumming of the need to come back here had vanished from my mind, leaving me with a sense of *rightness* that was un-nerving in its strength and made no sense at all.

I'd known I'd always loved the ocean, but this was taking it a bit far.

And I was really starting to suspect I might be insane.

Stepping from the bus into the cool midnight air of Santa Lucina, I tried to ignore the thought as I looked around the station. Other passengers climbed out behind me, heading for the compartments beneath the bus to gather their belongings. Heat from the exhaust cut through the salt on the wind, and drove me a few steps away from the enormous vehicle.

And then I saw Baylie.

I'd called her a couple hours ago to let her know I was coming. It seemed the smart thing to do, seeing as how I didn't have a ride, or even much of an idea how to get around town. But as I spotted her standing with Peter in the waiting area, I wondered if I shouldn't have tried to think of another plan. She looked upset.

And he looked pissed.

Bracing myself, I hefted my backpack and walked over to them.

"Hey," I said. "Thanks for coming."

"Young lady," Peter started. "What were you thinking?"

I swallowed.

"We've called your parents and left a message," he continued. "I'm sure they'll be on the way back here – *again* – as soon as they receive it."

I gave a chagrinned nod. That was probably true, assuming they hadn't just left for the coast the moment my dad got back to the motel, anyway.

"Don't you have anything to say?"

"I'm sorry?" I tried awkwardly. "Look, I know this is bad, I just…"

I trailed off. I didn't know what to tell him. I *had* to come back here. I didn't even feel like I'd had a choice in the matter. And now, although the sense of fishhooks nearly dragging me back had faded, the thought of leaving again instantly made them start to return.

But of course, that would just sound immature. Or, more

truthfully, psychotic.

He sighed. "Come on, it's late. We'll discuss this in the morning."

Moving past us, he walked toward the parking lot.

I glanced to Baylie. She didn't meet my eyes as she followed Peter.

A grimace twisting my face, I trailed after them.

The car ride back was silent, and when we reached the mansion, most of the house was dark. Leaving the car parked in the circle drive, Peter led the way inside. A single light was on in the kitchen, and the sound of someone setting a dish into the sink carried down the long hall.

"Goodnight," Peter said to us both as we came in.

"Yeah," Baylie said. She headed upstairs.

I hesitated. "Peter?"

"Yes?"

"Um, thanks for letting me come back here."

He gave me a patient look. "Of course. Now get some sleep."

I nodded and then followed Baylie. In the guest room, she was already climbing into her bed. I paused by the doorway, watching her.

"Are you mad at me?" I asked quietly.

She stopped moving. A heartbeat passed.

"No, I'm…" She shook her head, as if at a loss for words. "You really scared me. Taking off like that, getting on a bus back here. You could have been hurt."

"I know. I wasn't–"

"Why'd you do it?"

I didn't respond.

"Chloe?"

"I guess I just… freaked out. Mom and Dad were acting so weird – more than normal, I mean. They guarded the motel room door and watched me all night, even when I was asleep. And they told me they've decided to move to Salina, to stop 'bad influences'."

Her incredulity became confusion. "Wait. Me?"

I nodded.

"But now they're going to think I'm even more terrible."

"They think everything's terrible."

"Chloe!"

"I'm sorry, alright? I don't know what else to say."

I turned away, my gaze coming to rest on the darkness beyond the window. Light from the porch lamp covered the backyard, though the glow ended shy of the steps leading to the beach below.

"So now what are you going to do?" Baylie asked.

Shivering at the sudden compulsion to leave the house and head for the beach, I pulled my attention back to her. "Sleep? Peter's right. They'll be here to get me again soon."

"Yeah," she agreed distractedly. "But when they do… don't take off again, okay? I mean, maybe they'll calm down and decide not to move, if you give them a bit."

I regarded her dryly.

"Please?" she pressed. "I just... you scared me. Moving a couple hours away is one thing, and yeah, that'd suck. But I really don't want you to end up on the streets getting hurt or whatever."

There was something almost desperate in her voice. My brow furrowed.

She looked away. "There was a girl kidnapped around here last night."

I blinked. "What?"

"Homeless girl. Our age, though. She was hanging out with her friends by the pier, went to the restroom and never came back. But... one of Diane's friends is a reporter. The cops asked the news not to say anything yet, but she told Diane that they found blood at the scene. And it's just..." Baylie grimaced. "I know you're fine. You're here, you're fine, and I'm probably being ridiculous. But with that happening and with you out there on your own... I got worried."

I hesitated. "I'm sorry I scared you."

She nodded.

"And when they come back, I'll..." I shifted uncomfortably at the feeling of fishhooks sinking into my skin again. "I'll do my best not to take off."

"Thank you."

She gave me a small smile and then climbed into bed.

With an answering smile that really felt more like a grimace, I headed to my side of the room. I didn't know what else to tell her. Given the speed at which my parents apparently traveled, they'd probably be here within the hour. And no matter how much I didn't want to break my word to Baylie, if Mom and Dad tried to take me back with them, I didn't know if I'd be able to go.

The flutter of panic still lingering in my chest might not let me leave.

With a sickened feeling twisting my stomach, I changed into my pajamas and got into bed.

The sun pried my eyes open and for a moment, I lay in the bed staring up at the skylight, trying to hold onto the calm of my dreams. White clouds drifted past the narrow view overhead, and occasionally a seagull would sweep by, the bird's passage so fast I only registered it once it was gone.

My parents would probably be here today.

If they weren't already.

The thought frayed the last tendrils of my calm, making me scowl and setting my heart to racing again. Pulling my gaze from the blue sky, I shoved the blankets away and swung my legs over the side of the mattress. My backpack yielded up a pair of shorts and a shirt and, working desperately to keep my mind from dwelling on the realities the day would bring, I quickly changed into the clothes.

In the next bed, Baylie shifted beneath her blankets and opened her eyes.

"Morning," she said, her voice scratchy from sleep.

"Hey."

She drew a breath and then pushed the blankets back. "Sleep good?"

I shrugged. I'd spent the night not-drowning beneath miles of ocean, same as every other time I'd fallen asleep recently. It'd been wonderful and I'd never wanted to wake up.

And I hoped recurring dreams weren't a sign of madness too.

"Okay," I replied. "You?"

She nodded and grabbed her clothes from her own bag. I turned away, giving her privacy to get dressed.

"I was wondering," she continued when she was finished. "You want to head into town for some shopping? Maddox got a job at this cool old bookstore I wanted to show you."

I grinned. Bookstores were a weakness of mine, and the older the better. Over the years, stopping at them had been one of the few bright points on the absurd trips my parents had taken. "Yeah, that'd be great."

"Sweet," she said, smiling.

Tossing her pajamas back into her bag, she headed for the stairs, leaving me to follow.

The smell of breakfast permeated the first floor and the sound of the morning news carried from the end of the hall. Sunlight filled the dining room with the pearlescent glow that only morning possessed, and as we walked into the kitchen, the fresh sea air from the open windows joined the scent of baking.

But standing by the kitchen island, one hand to her mouth and her eyes locked on the countertop television, Diane seemed to see none of it.

I paused, and next to me, Baylie did the same. My gaze went from Diane to the screen, the words and images finally registering. A pair of scanned photographs were placed side-by-side, each of a different teenage girl with reddish-brown hair. Headlines about kidnappings played across the bottom of the screen, as well as a ticker displaying snippets of commentary from the police. The newscaster was listing off locations the girls had last been seen, one by the pier and the other in a neighborhood near the oceanfront, and asking anyone with information to call the hotline below.

"They could be sisters," Baylie whispered.

Diane jumped at the sound and then clicked off the television before turning around. "Girls. You're up."

She sounded breathless, and looked it too. Swallowing, she scanned her kitchen as though trying to remember what she'd been doing. "You want breakfast?"

"There's another girl missing?" Baylie asked.

Diane hesitated. "Yes."

"Was it like the last one? Did it look like she'd been hurt?"

"How did you—"

"I heard you and Peter in the front room last night, talking about what your reporter friend said."

Diane grimaced. "Marlene called half an hour ago. She

wanted Peter to ask the commissioner to speak with her. But… yes. They think it's the same people who took the last girl."

Baylie looked away.

Drawing a breath, Diane headed for the oven. "We'll just have to keep our eyes out for anything suspicious," she said, her assured tone sounding more than a bit forced, "and hope the police find some leads. But in the meantime… breakfast."

Retrieving a tray of scones, she set about transferring them to a cooling rack with a determination like she was restoring order to the world by that action alone. Beside me, Baylie looked like her appetite had long since fled, and I didn't feel far behind. But with the food presented to us, and Diane's almost adamant expression urging us on, we forced ourselves to eat.

Diane hovered nearby the entire time, as if worried someone would come into the kitchen to steal us away.

"You still want to go shopping?" I whispered to Baylie as Diane walked over to the sink with our empty plates.

"What?" Diane interrupted, turning back to us before Baylie could respond.

Baylie winced. "We were thinking of going to the bookstore where Maddox works."

Diane's gaze slid toward the black screen of the television, and something in her expression made me wonder what else Marlene had told her.

Baylie didn't seem to notice it, though. "We'll be careful," she insisted. "Please, Diane? We'll drive straight there and back again. He just told me about it yesterday, and I wanted to show Chloe the place before she had to head home."

Still looking hesitant, Diane set the plates in the sink.

"Have my parents called?" I asked into the silence. Whether or not Diane agreed to let us go, if they were only a few miles away, it'd all be a moot point.

"No, not yet."

My brow furrowed. "Really?"

"I'd feel better if you girls stayed here," Diane continued instead of answering.

"It's just a short trip," Baylie argued. "We'll bring Daisy, I've got pepper spray, and we won't talk to anyone but Maddox." She paused. "Please, Diane? This freaks me out too. Really. But we'll be super careful and if we stay here hiding all day, it's just going to drive me nuts."

"I–" Diane looked over as Noah walked into the kitchen.

"Morning," he said, and then he paused as if he'd picked up on the tension in the room. "Everything okay?"

"You can go if you take Noah with you," Diane said to Baylie.

Noah's eyebrows rose in surprise. "Huh?"

"Diane, we'll–" Baylie started.

"It's that or you stay home."

Baylie turned away, grimacing.

"What's going on?" Noah asked cautiously.

"Chloe and I were planning to head over to the bookshop

where Maddox works," Baylie explained. "But–"

"There was another kidnapping," Diane cut in. "And not to be anti-feminist or something, but I'd really prefer it if the girls weren't out there alone. So would you go with them?"

Seeming a bit uncomfortable, Noah looked between us all and then shrugged. "Yeah, sure."

"Good. Thank you."

Diane went back to the sink and turned on the water.

Noah eyed her skeptically and then glanced to me and Baylie. "You, uh, want to head out now?"

Baylie nodded and rose from her seat by the kitchen island. Not knowing what to say, I followed her and Noah out of the room. It only took a moment for me and Baylie to run upstairs and grab our things, and then we were on our way.

The store was just opening as Noah pulled the car to a stop, and the streets were mostly empty. In the park across the road, a few people sat finishing their morning coffee or talking on their cell phones. The bright sunlight made the shops along the street seem lively and inviting, and cool shadows beneath the store awnings added to the appeal. Leaving Baylie to tie Daisy's leash to a bike rack, I headed eagerly for the bookstore, happily noting the books propped on display stands in the window or, in one case, partially covered by the cat sleeping in front of it.

A ding rang out as Noah pulled open the door, and behind the counter, Maddox glanced up.

"Hey there," he called, smiling.

"Hi," Baylie said. She slipped past me to walk toward him.

I trailed after her, my eyes scanning the shelves.

There was something magical about places filled with books. An energy to being surrounded by so many words and ideas that whispered with each other and shouted at each other, that agreed and disagreed and contradicted each other. The combination created a pressure, a weight of presence that hinted at all the opinions and thoughts that made up the world, and that would take so much more than a lifetime to fully appreciate.

In a strange way, it bore a small similarity to the sea.

I wandered farther into the store, leaving Noah and Baylie chatting with Maddox by the register. Used books and new books alike crowded the shelves, and tables filled the space between the rows. I wound deeper into the store, skimming my gaze across the titles and covers and enjoying the fact that, besides one other store employee putting away books nearby, the early hour meant I was alone.

"Um… can I help you find something?"

I turned. One arm cradling a stack of books from his shelving cart, the employee eyed me questioningly.

"No thanks," I said, smiling. The guy looked like the staple of great bookstores everywhere: a pale-skinned, grad student type with messy hair and a rumpled tartan shirt who probably spent more time on books than personal grooming.

"Okay, well just let me know if you need anything."

I nodded and then went back to the books. A hardback

lying sideways on the shelf caught my eye and, grinning, I picked it up to put it in its proper place.

A shadow moved at the corner of my eye. I glanced toward it.

Something slammed into my head.

Red light and stars burst across my vision and then the sharp-edged shelves hit me, sending heat rushing down my face. The world tilted and the ground came next, and pain shot through my shoulder as it took the brunt of the impact with the thinly carpeted concrete.

A shadow fell between me and the glaring store lights, resolving into messy hair and brilliant blue eyes. Meaty flesh clamped over my mouth, pressing down on my lips and nose and choking out any chance of a scream. The other hand grabbed me, wrenching me up from the floor, and then a tartan-clad arm wrapped me, crushing my chest. I tried to break the grip, to move my arms and grab at his face or tear at his hair, but nothing was responding correctly and the black-ened blur of my vision was devouring everything.

"Hey!"

Baylie's shout was followed by an agonized scream, and suddenly the grip on me vanished. I plummeted down, hitting the ground hard enough to make the darkness swirl. Footsteps thudded past me, and more shouts came, while the ringing in my ears tried to smother everything in a rush of pain and white noise.

"Chloe? Chloe!"

Fabric pressed to the side of my face and instinctively, I jerked away. The blackness went to gray, and through the clouds, I saw Noah crouched beside me.

"Chloe, can you hear me?"

I opened my mouth to speak, and choked.

"Baylie's calling 911," he said. "EMTs will be here soon. Just stay still."

Noah looked up at something, and I tried to follow his gaze. By the stockroom door, Maddox appeared, his face flushed from running and his expression furious.

"Got away," he growled.

For a moment, he met Noah's eyes, saying nothing and through the fog, I couldn't read the exchange. But then Noah blinked and looked back down at me.

"Stay with me, okay?" he urged. "Just hang on."

I shivered. The ringing in my ears was getting louder, and blackness was creeping back across my gaze.

And everything hurt. God help me, everything hurt.

Blackness swelled. Weights pulled at my eyelids as the ringing grew louder, drowning the sound of Noah calling my name and dragging me down till darkness took the pain away.

❧ 8 ❧

ZEKE

It'd been a few days since I'd reached Santa Lucina and I was bored.

Really bored.

And I couldn't get that girl out of my mind.

For a while, I'd stayed near the ocean, wandering between the beach and the water while waiting to see if there was any change in the latter that would signal she'd returned. Nothing much had come of it, though. The town was on edge about something, and the tourists on the beach were less friendly than usual. Most met any questions I asked with muttered responses or suspicious replies, while a few had attempted to call the cops, seeming to find the fact I was looking for an auburn-haired girl something worth that level of alarm. After the third girl I'd tried to talk to had been hustled off by her friends – with plenty of wary glares in my direction – I'd given up and decided to head into town, just on the off chance I'd see anything.

Which was when I heard the ambulance.

I'd been walking past the downtown shops, enjoying the early morning and hoping to catch a glimpse of that girl or anyone who might've been with her, when the howl of sirens cut through the air. The sound drew closer and then an ambulance shot past the intersection in front of me in a blur of white sides and flashing lights. I followed, and found the vehicle pulling to a stop only a few hundred yards down the street.

I hung back, studying them from the corner. People rushed from the ambulance and ran into the store, while several others jogged to the back of the vehicle and threw open the doors to retrieve supplies. My brow furrowed as I watched them race in with a stretcher, and I wondered if I should just leave.

And then they hurried back outside.

It was the girl. She lay on the stretcher with blood covering her face and some kind of padded brace pinning her head, but it was her. The blond guy trailed the stretcher from the shop, with the other girl from the park clinging to his arm like it was the only thing keeping her standing. Police surrounded them, trying to ask questions, and then an older boy came out of the store, angrily interrupting the barrage with questions of his own.

The people loaded her into the back of the ambulance, the doors slammed and then they rushed to the front. The vehicle sped off.

I stared. She'd come back, obviously, or maybe she'd never

left, but now it looked like someone had attacked her.

And from the blood, they'd done a pretty good job of it too.

By the shop, the other girl was crying, while the older guy yelled something at the police about how the girl could die, so they needed to follow her.

A curse slipped from me in Yvarian before I could stop it. I didn't know what had happened and I didn't care. She was dehaian. She was possibly dying. It was true she was surrounded by humans, which was bizarre in itself and meant that if I brought any kind of help beyond what they'd understand, I was risking the exposure of our people, but dammit, she was in trouble. I couldn't just do *nothing*.

And I wasn't going to let this all end with 'and then some bastard killed her'.

I ran for the coast.

Streets blurred around me, taking too long to pass and stretching a million miles to the horizon. As the beach finally came into view, I swerved, avoiding the morning tourists and aiming for the most empty area I could manage. Wet sand sucked at my feet as I raced into the waves, and as the breakers rushed in, I dove, letting the water swallow me whole.

The change swept through me, dissolving the clothes I'd been too rushed to bother removing. Ignoring the debris, I kicked hard, rocketing forward and staying low so no trace of my fin broke the surface. The shallows sped by, and then I turned, racing for the supplies I'd hidden farther up the coast.

Minutes slid past, and for all my speed, the miles never

seemed to end.

I barely knew this girl.

Annoyed, I pushed the thought away. So I had to know someone in order to help them? Since when had *that* been a prerequisite of giving a damn?

The underwater portions of the cave came into view. Ducking inside, I swam up through the seawater that never dropped below the lower half of the place. Water-worn hollows and ledges scored the walls, and the sun didn't penetrate beyond the low archway that formed the entrance, providing countless shadowed hiding spaces. I drew up fast at the far end of the cave and started climbing, my tail becoming legs as I went.

My bag was where I'd left it a few days before, tucked into my usual hiding place on one of the uppermost ledges. Yanking it open, I scanned the contents, fear spiking for a moment at the thought I'd left the medicine behind when I'd packed.

And then I spotted the container at the bottom of the bag. Letting out a breath in relief, I sealed the bag again and then slung it over my shoulder, knowing I'd need the clothes inside when I returned to town. From the ledge, I dropped into the water and took off, racing back to Santa Lucina again.

I really hoped she didn't die before I got there.

Grimacing, I pushed myself to go faster. If she died, then I hadn't broken too many laws and Dad wouldn't be too pissed. And if she didn't, then the laws be damned, I'd have helped save her life. Dehaian medicine was powerful, drawing as it did on magic from deep beneath the water, and given how she'd looked at that store, the sieranchine in my bag was probably the best chance she had.

Assuming it didn't send her into shock and kill her, since that was its effect on non-dehaians and she wasn't exactly like anyone I'd ever seen.

I kicked harder, rocketing through the water. I'd be careful. Try a bit at first and see how she reacted. She *was* dehaian, even if she did weird things to the water. She should be fine.

The beach was annoyingly busy by the time I returned.

Glancing around beneath the waves, I hesitated, listening hard to the sounds from above the water, and then I darted toward what seemed like the least occupied stretch of sand. At a thought, my scales shed away, becoming legs and a dark imitation of swim trunks. Slipping from the water, I hurried up to the beach, hoping no one wondered why they hadn't seen me go into the water before I'd come back out – or why I had a bag over my shoulder in the ocean.

But I didn't have time to worry about it. She could be dying.

Jogging as fast as I dared over the sand, I fumbled a shirt and sandals from the bag, and then tugged them on as I headed for the street. At the stoplight, a cluster of people waited, several of whom eyed me skeptically when I hurried up.

"Where's the nearest hospital?" I asked the least tourist-looking one of them.

The woman blinked. "Hospital?"

"Yes, hospital. Where's the closest one?"

She hesitated, and then pointed. "A few miles that way."

The stoplight changed, and the walk symbol popped up.

"Thanks," I called as I took off running again.

Streets and miles and maddening stoplights passed, until at long last I rounded a corner and the white walls of the hospital came into view. Slowing, I adjusted the bag on my shoulder and strode inside.

It wasn't going to be easy to get near her.

I scowled, shoving the thought away. I'd figure something out.

Following the signs on the walls, I headed for the emergency department. The building was a maze, and if it hadn't been for the sense of the ocean behind me, I would have lost all awareness of direction by the time I reached the right place.

In the entryway, I hesitated. Across from me, a young brunette sat at a desk with brass letters overhead that marked the area as reception. A pair of large sliding doors to my right led to the outside – an entrance I hadn't seen at all when I'd reached the building, but that I'd damn well use to get out of this labyrinth once I was done. In the glass-walled waiting area nearby, the two guys from the store sat, casting annoyed glances to the television I could hear playing in the room and looking as though they could barely keep from pacing. An older man and a police officer were with them, the latter of whom was still asking questions from the look of it, though the pair who'd driven her away in a car several days before were nowhere to be seen. Another cop stood by the double doors to my left that blocked off the remainder of the emergency department.

His gaze slid toward me. I looked away.

"Can I help you?" the woman behind the desk asked.

I hesitated. I couldn't hope to sneak past them all.

"Yeah, um..." I glanced to the cop again, and tried to keep my voice low. "I'm here to see the girl who was brought in a bit ago. The one who'd been hit in the head?"

"And you are?"

"A friend."

The caution on her face was blatant. "Well, I'm sorry, but she already has visitors and only two people are allowed to see a patient at a time."

"I won't be in the way. Please, I just want to check on her."

She glanced to the police officer by the doors and then back to me. "I told you. No more than two visitors at a time. Now, if you want to wait, I'll need to see some identification. Otherwise..."

Her eyebrow raised pointedly.

I looked back at the cop. Identification was out of the question and waiting wouldn't do any good. The girl could be dying. I only needed a few uninterrupted seconds to maybe change that.

Slowly, I let out a breath. There was one way. It was illegal. And wrong. But if I only used a little, the woman would most likely be fine and recover long before anything turned life-threatening.

And I could really be running out of time.

Trying not to feel like a bastard, I turned back to her and smiled. "Listen," I glanced down at her name tag. "Becky? I, um…"

I reached out fast, taking her hand. Her brow drew down in alarm and she jerked back, attempting to pull away, but the small twist of magic had already touched her skin.

Her expression flickered with confusion, and then melted into the sort of adoration that only the truly sick among us dehaians would enjoy.

I made myself keep smiling as I let the magic carry through my voice as well. "I need to get in there. Can you open the door?"

She frowned, still fighting it, and then her head twitched in a nod. Her hand fumbled for the button, and the doors swung back to let me through.

"Thank you," I said, feeling nauseated.

The police officer watched me as I walked past. A desk formed the corner of two adjoining halls ahead, and beside it, I could see the girl from the store and another woman, both of them talking anxiously to a doctor. Curtains enclosed the space behind them, though a second later, a nurse pushed the fabric aside to carry out a tray, revealing the girl lying on a bed.

I hesitated. I could feel the police officer's gaze still on my back, and if I headed straight for her, he'd be certain to stop me. But another curtained area was not too far away, and through a gap in the fabric, I could see that it was empty.

Trying to look purposeful, I marched inside. A few heartbeats passed, and then I leaned my head out again.

The cop had turned back toward the waiting room, and the doors were swinging closed behind him. I looked to the women and the doctor. He was taking them to a lighted wall panel farther down the adjoining corridor, where transparent black sheets showed side views of a human skull.

I strode down the hall and slid into the curtained space holding the girl.

She looked like hell. Tubes ran from her nose and arms to plastic bags on wheeled poles and beeping machines on the wall. Beneath the bandages wrapping her head, one side of her face was puffy, the skin blue and purple and red in turns, and the other side bore a vicious gash surrounded by swelling of its own.

I couldn't keep myself from staring as I crossed to her bedside. It didn't make sense. She electrocuted the water, yes. She wasn't like anyone I'd ever seen, dehaian or otherwise.

But why would someone do *this* to her?

Exhaling sharply, I forced myself to focus. Reaching into my bag, I tugged out the container of sieranchine and then thumbed the lid from its top. With a quick glance to the curtain enclosing us, I pulled a shirt out as well. Covering my fingers with the fabric, I scooped the shimmering gel out before setting the container on the wheeled stand nearby. Turning her arm over gently, I wiped the wet shirt across the inside of her arm, testing her reaction.

Her skin glistened, gaining a hint of golden iridescence that faded almost as quickly as it had come.

But she didn't go into shock or show any sign of a negative response.

I doused the shirt with medicine again and swiped it across her face and neck and every bit of uncovered skin I could reach.

She stirred on the bed with a soft sigh.

I stepped away and shoved the t-shirt and container back into my bag. My skin tingled as a bit of the sieranchine touched it, and hastily, I wiped my hand on my shirt. I'd probably end up with a killer headache just from that contact – strong really was an understatement for that stuff – but that was a problem for later.

Her bruises were already diminishing. The gash on her cheek seemed less red, and the swelling appeared to be going down.

I let out a breath and then glanced to the curtain again. She'd be alright. I'd still get answers to all my questions – eventually, anyway – and she'd be alright.

Now for getting out of here.

Cautiously, I peered around the edge of the curtain. By the lighted panel, the women and the doctor still discussed something. Slipping across the adjoining hall, I walked quickly back toward the waiting area and past the cop, heading for the exit.

Across the room, the doors to the outside opened. An ambulance sat in the driveway, its lights flashing, while doctors rushed by the sliding door, a stretcher with an old man on it between them and a dozen other people trailing behind.

All of whom were now blocking my path.

"H-hey wait," Becky called to me from the reception desk, her voice vague with confusion. "You weren't... you shouldn't have been..."

My heart hit my throat and I made a sharp turn for the hall that I'd taken through the hospital a few minutes before. I'd really held back earlier. The effects were wearing off faster than I'd expected.

Which meant Becky would be fine and that was great.

Except now she was calling out to the cop.

I rounded the corner, barely keeping from running as I retraced my steps to the main exit. I hadn't seen any police near the hospital entrance, but that didn't mean he wouldn't call any to come stop me. I'd just been in the water, and thus could probably handle even two or three weeks out of it, but that wouldn't fix all the other issues being taken into custody would create.

There had to be another way out of here.

I strode down the hall, cursing the hospital maze.

"Hey you!"

I didn't look back. Through a glass door ahead, I could see daylight and I hurried toward it. Footsteps pounded down the hall behind me. I shoved the crossbar on the door and rushed out into the fresh air.

And then I ran.

I could hear the cop shouting, first at me and then into his radio, but I'd already reached the corner. Veering around the turn, I took off down the next street. Intersections appeared and fell behind me in rapid succession, and people stumbled away in surprise as I sped by. Over the whistle of the wind in my ears, I listened for sirens, grateful not to hear any until I'd finally reached the road opposite the beach.

And by then, it was really too late for them.

I dashed across the sand and into the water, leaving Santa Lucina behind.

9

CHLOE

I woke to the sound of beeping and the feeling of way too
many pillows under my back. The smell of antiseptic stung
my nose and the air had a strange dryness that I couldn't place.
Wincing at the glare of sunlight, I opened my eyes.

Medical equipment stood next to me, and I was lying on a
bed surrounded by metal rails. Baylie was curled in an armchair
nearby, her face red as though she'd been crying, while Diane
sat near her, one hand rubbing Baylie's shoulder. On the far
side of the room, Noah and his dad were talking with a gray-
haired doctor.

My brow furrowed in confusion. I'd been at the bookstore.
We'd gone to see Maddox. I'd walked back to check out the
books and …

I looked back at the doctor.

"–amazing improvement, considering her earlier condi-
tion," he was saying in a low voice. "If she wakes up soon, we
should–"

"Hey," Baylie interrupted, catching sight of me. She shoved away from the armchair and hurried to the bedside, relief clear on her face.

Noah and the others turned around. Stepping past them, the doctor came over.

"Hello," he said. "My name is Doctor Michaelson. How are you feeling?"

I hesitated. "My head hurts."

He nodded understandingly. "You had a bit of an accident. Your head was hit. I'd like to ask you a few questions, though, just to test how your memory is doing. Is that alright?"

Behind him, I saw Noah look away, muscles working beneath his jaw, while Diane had entangled her fingers so tightly together, her knuckles were white.

"Okay..." I allowed.

"Could you tell me your full name?"

"Chloe Marie Kowalski."

He smiled. "When's your birthday, Chloe?"

"August twelfth."

"Just in time for school, eh?"

"Yeah."

His smile remained. "Now, what can you tell me about what happened to you, Chloe? What do you remember?"

I paused. We'd been at the bookstore. I'd been walking around, one of the employees had asked if I needed anything, and...

I drew a sharp breath. Something had happened. Something

bad.

Shaking my head, I shied away from the memory. "I-I don't…"

"It's okay," the doctor interjected. He glanced back at the others. "It might start coming back in a bit. Don't push it."

I swallowed. Everyone else looked worried. Or angry. Really, *really* angry.

"What happened?" I pressed.

They all looked to the doctor. He hesitated a moment, and then nodded.

"One of the store employees went psycho," Noah said, his voice nearly a growl. His father put a hand to his shoulder, and Noah gritted his teeth, looking away.

"He attacked you," Baylie supplied, sounding choked. "He just—"

"The police think he was one of the people involved in those kidnappings," Diane continued for her. "And since you… well, honey, you look a bit like the other girls who are missing. The police think he must've believed he had the opportunity to take you too. But now that they know who he is, they're searching his house, and they have people looking for him everywhere. He won't get away."

I stared at her.

"That's probably enough for now," the doctor said. "You're safe here, Chloe. That's the important thing. So now I just want you to focus on getting well."

Feeling like he was nuts, I didn't say anything. Someone

had attacked me? And now I was supposed to forget that?

He'd grabbed my mouth.

The memory flashed through my head, vivid and clear.

He'd put his arm around my chest and dragged me up from the ground. I hadn't been able to fight him. I'd wanted to; he'd just been so strong.

So incredibly strong.

"Chloe," the doctor said.

I blinked, my heart racing as I looked back at him.

"You're safe."

Swallowing, I nodded.

He gave me an understanding smile. "Your friends are going to stay here with you, alright? And if you keep doing this well, we'll have you home in a few days."

"Okay," I said.

He patted my arm and then headed for the door. Peter followed him out.

Diane came over to the bed. "Get some sleep, honey. You're doing really well, but the doctor says sleep could help you more than anything."

I glanced from her to Baylie and Noah. "They didn't catch him?"

Diane hesitated. "They will. But the doctor's right. We're all going to be here. He won't get near you again." She put a hand to my shoulder. "Just sleep."

My brow furrowed, but I turned my face toward the pillow, trying to do as she asked. Truth was, though, I wasn't tired.

Not really. Instead, I just felt tingly, like between all the medicines the doctors had probably given me, I could almost feel my body fixing itself.

And I didn't want to close my eyes anyway.

I watched the window. The others wouldn't let him near me. I knew that. I hated relying on them for protection, hated being this scared, but I knew they'd keep me safe.

Though it wasn't like any of us could have known the guy was somebody to fear.

I drew a breath, working to stay calm like everyone had ordered.

He'd just looked so *ordinary*. Awkward and pale, maybe, like a frail bookworm who spent more time reading than he did with girls or out in the sun. But mostly, he'd just seemed like a normal guy.

And when he'd grabbed me, he'd been anything but. Strong. So stupidly strong, with his face twisted like he'd hated me with everything in his being. And his eyes...

I shivered, the memory coming back.

They'd changed. Not at first, but as he grabbed me, the watery color had transformed.

Into brilliant, glowing blue.

Just like the boy from the ocean.

I climbed from the car into the late afternoon sunlight, and tried to ignore the way everyone watched me to see if I'd fall. It'd been three days since I'd ended up in the hospital, and finally Doctor Michaelson had given his okay for me to go home.

It couldn't have come too soon. I appreciated all that the hospital staff had done and everything, but if I had to spend one more minute being watched and checked and worried over, I thought I'd lose my mind.

Though everyone here was still doing that.

Shutting the door behind me, I headed for the house. Whatever damage the bookstore guy – Maddox told us his name was Jesse, though from the way he said the man's name now, he made it sound like a curse – had done to me seemed to have healed. I wasn't dizzy and my head only occasionally ached. For all intents and purposes, I was fine.

Which the doctor thought was incredible.

And I didn't care.

Jesse had hit me really hard, it was true, and the bookshelves had as well. There'd been a lot of blood, or so I gathered from the looks on Baylie and Noah's faces whenever the topic of the stitches on my forehead came up, and some kind of swelling that'd since disappeared. But now I was fine. My trip to Santa Lucina had been filled with nothing but drama – loads and *loads* of drama – but now... now I was fine.

And I'd keep anything else weird from happening if I had to lock myself in the guest room.

Fighting off a scowl at the thought, I followed Peter inside.

Diane and Baylie hovered near me, worry practically radiating from them, while Noah trailed after us, one hand on his cell phone as he conferred with Maddox, who'd been covering shifts at the bookstore since Jesse disappeared. I hoped we'd just be able to have a quiet evening, doing nothing if at all possible. I wanted one day of normalcy in this place. It'd give me something nice to remember, compared to everything else.

Especially since my parents could show up at any time.

The scowl tried to return. Dad left a message with the Delaneys the day before, saying nothing beyond the fact they would be back soon. He gave no reason for what had taken them so long, though given that they hadn't looked good the last time I'd seen them, it worried me. But meanwhile, they were apparently on their way.

And so I waited.

"Go ahead and have a seat in the living room," Diane said to me as the front door closed. "Would you like some iced tea?"

"That's okay. Thank you, though. I'm just going to go upstairs, if that's alright?"

She looked worried.

I gave her something approaching a smile and then headed to the second floor, working to ignore the concern that followed me like a cloud. I didn't want to leave when my parents came back – the panicked, fishhook feeling returned at the thought – but staying here was starting to become just as uncomfortable.

The guest room was blessedly quiet. Sinking onto the bed, I looked to the window, watching the blue water and the equally blue horizon.

"Hey."

I turned. By the door, Baylie stood, watching me nervously.

"Hey," I replied, feeling guilty for the way I wanted to grimace at her expression.

"You alright?" she pressed.

A bit of the grimace slipped through.

She winced. "Sorry."

Her gaze dropped to the floor.

"What is it?" I asked.

She hesitated, and then crossed the room and sat down on the bed next to mine.

"I just..." She glanced to the open doorway. "I feel so bad about what happened."

My brow furrowed.

"I was the one who insisted we go," she explained, a touch desperately. "I knew those girls were missing and I should have thought–"

"What? That the psycho who kidnapped them worked at the bookstore?"

She looked pained.

"Baylie, seriously. It wasn't your fault."

Footsteps in the hall made me turn. Noah paused outside the door, looking between us with concern.

"You guys doing okay?"

"Fine," I said, struggling to keep from snapping simply because I was tired of the question. "Baylie and I were... talking."

I wasn't sure what else to tell him. I didn't want to embarrass her.

For a moment, Noah studied Baylie, and something in his expression made me think he guessed what the conversation had been about anyway.

"She tell you about the pepper spray?" he asked me.

Confused, I shook my head.

He lifted an eyebrow at his stepsister. Baylie grimaced.

"She was the first to see what the guy was doing," Noah explained when she didn't say anything. "She pepper-sprayed him. Made him let you go."

The memory came back. "I heard someone scream."

Noah nodded. "You need to stop blaming yourself," he told Baylie.

She looked down.

"Baylie," I said. "Please? It's not your fault." I paused. "You probably saved my life."

She swallowed, her face taking on the same green cast I'd seen for days, whenever she or the others thought back on what things must have looked like in the bookstore.

I turned to the window, determinedly ignoring the expression.

"He was just so..." Baylie trailed off.

"Insane," I supplied, attempting to keep my voice even as I

glanced back at them.

Noah's face made it clear he thought the same, possibly with a few more colorful words thrown in.

"But I'm *fine*," I continued. "Really."

Baylie hesitated a moment, and then nodded.

"So you want to go shopping again?" I asked.

Incredulous, she looked up at me. I grinned.

She made an exasperated noise, but a smile tugged at her lips. "I swear, you'd tell jokes in the middle of anything."

Holding onto the grin, I pushed to my feet, though her words weren't quite true.

I was just going to be fine if it killed me.

"Okay, so no shopping," I said, my tone lighter than I actually felt. "What else can we do? Volleyball? Maybe a game or something?"

They hesitated.

"Come on," I said, almost feeling ready to beg. "Let's do something normal, okay?"

"You play poker?" Noah asked.

"No, but I'll learn."

He smiled.

By the bed, Baylie took a breath, almost visibly pushing her concern back inside. "Watch out, though. He's vicious."

Noah gave her a mock glare.

We headed for the stairs again, and this time, Baylie intercepted Diane before she could worry at me further. Noah grabbed a deck of cards from an end table in the living room, and in short order we were set up to play.

Hours passed and by the time dinner rolled around, I'd managed to win a few hands. We took a brief break to eat and then went back to the game, with Maddox joining us after he returned from work.

And for a while, I finally felt like life was normal.

It was late when we called it quits, and Diane and Peter had long since gone to bed. Waving goodnight to the guys, Baylie and I headed back to our room. As she climbed beneath the covers, I pulled open the window to let in the cool night air, and when I turned back around, I realized she'd already fallen asleep.

I grinned as I changed into my pajamas and then got into bed. She'd stayed awake at the hospital for days; it was about time the girl got some rest. The pillow felt good beneath my head as I lay down, and on the ceiling, the skylight showed a beautiful view of the stars.

But sleep didn't want to come.

It'd been like this ever since the first night in the hospital. Lying around all day meant I didn't use much energy, and so when it came time to sleep, I simply couldn't. My whole body wouldn't stop buzzing.

Rolling over, I closed my eyes, trying to will myself into unconsciousness. Time crawled by, my mind dipping briefly into confusing dreams about the previous day before surfacing again. The soothing ocean was nowhere to be found, and my muscles wouldn't stop twitching.

I scowled, pushing away from the bed and looking around the room. Maybe if I walked around the house for a while, or got something warm to drink, I'd finally be able to sleep. But anything was better than lying here all night, gradually turning into a cramped ball of nervous energy.

Leaving the room silently, I walked down the hall. The air was heavy and still, and carried the slightly unsettling sense of people sleeping all around me – people who might wake up if I was too loud. Wincing at the stairs, I crept to the first floor, doing my best to avoid making the steps creak.

The kitchen tile was cold beneath my bare feet, and through the windows of the dining room, the moon bathed the whole space in silver light. By the doorway, I paused, suddenly captivated by the sight of the bluffs and the water beyond.

And I headed for the back door.

The brass lock gave soundlessly as I flipped it over. I pulled open the door, cool air blowing past me into the kitchen, and then tugged it closed as I stepped out onto the chilled concrete of the patio. The sound of the waves grew louder as I crossed the grass to the stairway and then descended the steps to the beach.

At the base of the stairs, I paused, caught by the urge to just walk into the waves, as though the ocean in my dreams and delusions would be the same as the black water in front of me. My hand gripped the railing as I struggled against the feeling, knowing that down where no one could see me and while the whole family was asleep, there was no way that a midnight swim could possibly be a good plan.

A moment passed. The compulsion faded. Swallowing hard, I sank onto the wooden steps. Drawing a shaky breath of the salty air, I wrapped my arms around my knees and watched the waves.

The hairs on my skin rose.

My brow furrowed at the sudden sense I wasn't alone. Heart pounding, I took the rail and pulled myself to my feet, getting ready to jog back up the stairs.

"Hello," came a familiar voice.

My gaze snapped to the right. From a shadowed pile of rocks at the base of the bluffs, a form stepped out into the moonlight.

The boy from the ocean.

I retreated a step, cursing my stupidity at coming out here in my pajama shorts and t-shirt, and leaving Baylie's pepper spray in the house.

He paused. The moonlight shone on his black hair, the strands glistening wetly like he'd just come from the water, and below his smooth chest, he only wore a pair of dark swim trunks. His brow drew down at the sight of my caution, and he held up his hands peaceably.

"I'm not going to hurt you," he said as if confused why I thought that would be the case.

I didn't move.

"I just wanted to talk," he continued in the same tone.

"Why?" I hesitated. "Who are you?"

"I was going to ask you that."

My foot moved back a step.

"Okay, sorry. I just…" He shook his head. "You can call me Zeke. And you are?"

"Why're you watching me?"

He paused. "You're different."

My brow furrowed.

"From me," he elaborated. "The rest of us."

My expression didn't change.

Frustration twisted his face for a heartbeat. "Look, I've already broken like… a dozen laws by helping you back at the hospital, and being here isn't doing me much good either. But I see you living here like a human, I felt what you did to the water the other night, and I saw what happened the next day too. I'd *love* to know what's going on, so…"

I stared.

"You want to give me some help here?" he finished. "I'm just trying to figure this out."

My heart was pounding so hard, it felt like it was crushing my chest. Shaking, I backed up another step.

"Look," he said, starting forward.

I gasped, my hand coming up defensively, and he froze.

"Stay away from me," I warned.

"I know what you are, okay? I just want to know what you did."

"Come any closer, and I scream enough to wake the town, you get me?"

"I told you. I'm not going to hurt you."

A scoff escaped me.

He paused. "I mean it. I only want to know how you did it. How…" He gestured carefully to the top of the bluffs. "Well, any of this, really."

I didn't have a clue what to say. He was insane, that much was obvious. Insane… and able to speak to me underwater. While swimming God knew how deep too.

Trembling, I swallowed. "What are you?"

"Dehaian," he replied. My expression stayed the same, and his lip twitched. "You know. Fish. Same as you."

My head shook. "I… you're…"

The words refused to come. My legs were unsteady beneath me, and if not for the edge of the wooden rail biting into my palm, I'd have believed I was dreaming.

Though given how vivid my dreams had been lately, there was still a good chance.

"I'm not…" I tried. The words still wouldn't come. They were too stupid. Too insane. I wasn't going to argue about whether or not I was a *fish*. "You stay away from me," I said instead. "From the house, from anywhere. I see you again, I'm calling the cops."

He hesitated. "I saw you underwater. I saw you changing. I know what you are."

"I'm human, you freak!" I yelled, my voice breaking.

Gasping, I started up the stairs.

"Then why'd the sieranchine work on you in the hospital?"

I froze. Turning, I looked back to where he stood at the base of the stairway.

"I snuck into the hospital," he said. "I used some of our medicine on you, in case it'd help." He paused. "It did."

On the banister, my hand shook. Amazing recovery, the doctor had called it. A sudden and swift turnaround from when they'd brought me in. He'd been stunned.

And I'd just felt like I had enough energy to fly to the moon.

"Why'd you do that?" I managed.

He shrugged a shoulder, not answering.

"Do you know where Jesse is?"

His brow furrowed. "Who?"

"The guy at the bookstore."

"I don't know any guy at the bookstore."

"He attacked me."

"I don't–"

"He looked like you."

Zeke paused. "How?"

"His eyes."

He shook his head. "We don't work in bookstores. We don't work at all, for that matter. Not on land." He hesitated. "And you should know that."

I turned to go up the stairs again.

"You really don't have any idea what I'm talking about, do you?" he called.

"I know you're crazy," I snapped over my shoulder.

"You're telling me you don't feel the pull of the water? You don't have to be near it? Anything?"

I stopped and looked back at him.

"We don't do well far from the ocean," he said. "We get sick if we're away for too long." He paused. "That doesn't happen to you?"

I swallowed. "Just lately," I whispered.

A heartbeat passed, and he stepped back from the base of the stairway, clearing a path from me to the water's edge.

"I'm not a threat to you," he said. "I swear. I just want answers. I didn't mean to scare you."

I didn't move.

"Can we start over?" he asked.

My shoulder lifted in a small shrug.

"Okay. Like I said, I'm Zeke. And you are?"

"Chloe."

His lip twitched, wry humor in his blue eyes. "Nice to meet you, Chloe. You ever heard of dehaians?"

Not taking my eyes from him, I shook my head.

"Alright. Can I show you then?"

He gestured to the ocean. Cautiously, I descended the stairs. Keeping well clear of him, I walked to the edge of the wet sand.

"It helps if you're in the water," he said, a trace of amusement entering his voice.

I stayed where I was.

"Okay," he amended, humor fading. "Just... have a seat."

Still watching him, I sank onto the sand.

He crouched several feet away, his lean-muscled arms braced on his knees and his bare skin bright in the moonlight. "Put your legs out so the water hits them. And don't fight it."

My brow furrowed, but I stretched my legs out.

He glanced to the ocean. A moment passed as the tide swept out and then came rolling back in.

Water rushed up around my legs, cool and fast and wonderful, and my skin tingled as it passed. My lips twitched reflexively toward a smile, and I fought the expression, not wanting to give any sign of how great it felt.

I looked back to him as the water pulled away again.

His mouth tightened. "Okay, listen, how about this? I'm not crazy, alright? Let's agree on that first off. Oh, and that I don't want to hurt you. Because that's true too. So now if you'll just tell me—"

The tide hit me and I gasped, unprepared for it. Water swept up around my feet, my knees, my thighs and sent shivers running through every inch of my body. I gulped down a breath, my hands bracing me on the sand as the shock passed.

And he chuckled, as if he'd meant to distract me all along.

I glared, but his amusement just grew. He seemed incapable of keeping it away.

"Don't freak," he warned.

He pointed. My gaze followed.

I choked on the air.

Something was wrong with my legs. Really wrong. For one

thing, they were shimmering, and not in some fancy, mineral lotion kind of way. Iridescent hints of blue and green, yellow and orange shone from my thighs to my feet. And for another, they were covered in a strange, barely perceptible texture.

Texture like scales.

Instinctively, my hands moved to swipe it away and then I froze, fear catching up with me. I didn't want to touch it. I didn't want to feel this on me.

I lifted my foot, and choked all over again. Thread-like filaments no thicker than a hair ran from one leg to the next, glistening in the same way as my skin, though they snapped when I moved and faded into the moonlight like smoke.

The tide rolled toward me again. Pushing at the sand, I scooted awkwardly back from it, watching the water like it was acid till it finally rushed away.

Trembling, I looked at Zeke.

"What'd you do to me?" I whispered.

"Nothing. You're dehaian. It's fine."

I stared at him.

He took a breath. "Sorry. Okay. I just… You're like me. You get under the water and you *don't* fight it, you start changing like this. I saw you begin doing it the other day. And it's fine. It's not anything. It's just who you are."

"Y-you saw…"

I couldn't finish, but he just nodded. My head shook in response.

"But I didn't… I…"

"You were breathing underwater. For goodness sake, you were screaming. That's how I found you. Any dehaian would have heard that for miles. And yeah, you were."

I swallowed hard. "Wh-what was I…"

His brow furrowed, and then he seemed to get the question, even if I couldn't bring myself to say it.

"Just the other way we get around," he answered, his lip curving back into that annoying, amused smile. "We… well, the way you are on land? That's only one option."

He grinned. "Mermaid, Chloe. That's what humans would call you. Or, you know, merman for me. But yeah, that. We prefer our own terms, though."

I blinked. I wanted to run back to the house. Or wake up. Either would've been great.

But I couldn't even breathe.

"You aren't like them," he said. "You're one of us. You come into the water with me now, I'll prove it to you."

I shoved away from the sand, my body finally answering the frantic signals from my brain. And then I fell back again as my legs crumpled.

Zeke rose and I scrambled backward to stay away from him. He froze.

"Don't," I warned. "Just… don't."

I looked down at my legs. The texture and the shine were mostly gone, leaving only a faint shimmer like salt drying on my skin.

Shivers ran through me.

"It's hard to switch back if you're not used to it," he explained. "Give it a minute."

I eyed him warily.

He eased back into a crouch several feet away. "It's better if you let yourself change fully, though. Like this... the energy kind of builds. Makes it harder to stay on land."

I shook my head quickly, hearing the suggestion behind the words.

"Okay," he allowed. "But can you tell me how you've managed to keep out of the ocean this long? If you've never... you know, done any of this before?"

I swallowed. "I live in Kansas."

His brow furrowed. "That's one of the middle states, right?"

I stared at him.

"What?" he protested. "You know the provinces of Teariad? Ryaira?"

I hesitated. "One of the middle ones, yeah."

He watched me for a moment. "Okay. And you've lived there since...?"

"My whole life."

His eyebrows rose and fell in amazement. "I can't even... there's no way you should have been able to do that."

My shoulder twitched in a shrug. "I wanted to come here. My parents just hate water. They wouldn't let me."

"Your parents," he repeated. "They hate water."

I nodded.

"So they're not... I mean... they can't be..."

He looked like he couldn't find the right words.

"They got sick just being near the ocean."

"Really?" he said. A doubtful expression crossed his face as his gaze dropped to the sand.

I looked down. My muscles didn't feel as shaky and carefully, I pushed to my feet. He glanced up, and then stood as well.

"I'm going to guess your friends aren't like you, either, right?" he said.

My gaze twitched to the top of the bluffs. "I'm human," I told him. "We... we're all human."

His brow furrowed, but I just headed for the stairs.

"Chloe," he called.

I paused, not looking back.

"You're not," he said. "And it's going to be hard, trying to stay like this. Harder now than it was before."

He hesitated. "But it doesn't have to be. We can help you. And if you've found a way to be on the land like you have... maybe you could help us too."

Trembling, I glanced back at him. "Stay away from me, Zeke. Please."

I took to the stairs, leaving him standing on the moonlit beach.

The house was still around me as I came inside, and when I reached the bedroom, I found Baylie still asleep. Nothing had changed in all the time I'd been outside.

Except everything.

I changed into dry pajamas and then slid beneath the blankets, fighting to hold back tears at the scratchy feeling of sheets that had been soft on my skin only a short while ago. A cool breeze twisted through the window, carrying the smell of the ocean and the sound of the waves on the shore.

And I got up again and tugged the window closed.

I returned to bed, pulling the blankets up to my chin. Shivering from more than the night air, I squeezed my eyes closed and prayed I'd wake tomorrow to find this had all been a dream.

❧ 10 ❧

ZEKE

I watched her walk away and tried not to swear.

That'd gone well.

I scowled. I'd never even *considered* she didn't know what she was. I mean, how could anyone have missed that their entire life? And yet, from everything I'd seen of her reactions, it seemed like that was exactly what'd happened. She'd never heard of dehaians. She had no idea how she'd stayed on land this long.

She had no clue that she'd basically electrocuted the ocean a few days ago.

And now she didn't want me anywhere near her.

Which was just great.

I turned back to the water, shaking my head at myself. I was being fatalistic, and impatient too. If she'd actually never heard of us, finding out like this would probably be a shock. So maybe she just needed a bit to let it sink in. Maybe she'd come around and we could talk about whatever it was she'd done to the water, and about how she'd managed to remain on land all these years in a place none of us could even reach.

And about how there was no way her parents were dehaians.

Seawater swallowed me as I dove back into the waves. I hadn't known how to say it. How did you tell that to someone, especially someone you'd met only a few minutes before? Your parents can't be your parents. Getting sick around water wasn't remotely something that happened to us.

Of course, neither was staying on land for your whole life. Or living in Kansas.

An annoyed sound escape me. Endless layers of questions, and I was no closer to finding an answer to any of them than I'd been before. Instead, I'd just managed *yet again* to frighten the pretty girl who electrocuted the ocean.

Chloe.

My lip twitched. That was a bright side. At least now I knew her name.

I dove lower as the seafloor dropped, my innate magic compensating for the increase in pressure. I'd give her a day or so. See if she came around. It was all I could do anyway.

A shadow shot through the water in front of me.

I pulled up, my vision sharpening further and my eyes tracking the path the dark shape had followed. My senses stretched, trying to pick out any change in the water nearby.

I felt a ripple in the water below me. I darted to the side.

It was too late.

Something slammed into my tail, and suddenly, tentacle-ropes were crawling all over me, sprouting like weeds one from the other and wrapping around my body at high speed. I twisted, trying to break free, when another blast struck my side, adding more sucker-laden tentacles to the mess.

Places on the seafloor flickered, the sense of emptiness there suddenly giving away to dehaians who'd been hiding behind camouflaging veils. The dehaians rushed upward and surrounded me, while another came to a stop directly in front of me.

He held a rock in his hand. I thrashed at the restraints. He swung.

Everything went black.

"...*promised* him that the boy would not be harmed, under-stand?"

The words drifted through the throbbing blur of the world.

"Yes, Wisdom."

My brow furrowed and then I opened my eyes.

I was upright. I was still underwater. And my forearms were encased in thick shackles bound to chains driven deep into the wall.

Gritting my teeth against the pounding of my head, I looked up.

Two dozen dehaians were watching me, each of them easily

several years or more my age.

And they didn't exactly look friendly.

A large cave surrounded them, three hundred feet across with a ceiling at least a hundred feet high. The middle of the floor vanished into a deep pit over which the dehaians hovered, while farther behind them the cave became a tunnel leading into darkness. Water-torches glowed atop metal poles driven into the rock, their flames shimmering with blue and white light, while on the far left side of the space, more torches flanked a stone slab that almost looked like an altar.

My gaze caught on the restraints bolted to the rock, and then rose to the mosaic on the wall behind it. In intricate detail, gemstones picked out a twisted symbol, the shape like a cage of barbed wire encircling an opalescent star.

Disbelief moved through me, followed swiftly by fear.

It wasn't possible. It shouldn't have been possible. They'd died. A century ago, their cult had been wiped out in one of the only acts that had united every nation in the dehaian world.

Because they'd been completely insane.

From the center of their group, one of the dehaians came closer, and by the way the others pulled back to give him room, it didn't take a genius to figure out he was in charge. His hair was silver and his scales were too. He looked old enough to be my grandfather, and his dark eyes sent shivers down my spine.

They seemed to cut right through me, and leave cloying

fingerprints over all they saw.

"Hello," the man said in Yvarian, his voice calm as the ocean on a windless day.

I pulled at the shackles, but the damn things wouldn't budge.

"I am Wisdom Kirzan," he continued in the same tone. "High Priest of the Sylphaen. Welcome to the fourth sanctum of our faith. I apologize that we have to meet this way, and that we have been forced to place you in such accommodations. I do hope, however, that you will believe me when I say the restraints are for your protection. We do not understand one another yet. This may lead you to act rashly and cause the acolytes to undertake protective measures in response. I would hate for that to happen, as I have great faith you will see the light."

My skin crawled as his lips curved into a smile like he knew something about me that I didn't.

Like he could already see me on his side.

"I know you have been taught to fear us. To believe the Sylphaen are the monsters of old tales. Yet your homeland of Yvaria prides itself on hearing both sides of a case, correct? On giving fair weight to all arguments before making a decision? So what of us? Are you not brave enough to hear ours?"

At my silence, Kirzan sighed.

"Have you not wondered why our people live as they do? Hidden beneath the waves, shrouding themselves with magic for fear of notice by the human world? Has it never bothered you that we, with such power, should cower in fear of creatures so much weaker than ourselves?"

I didn't answer. It was a stupid question anyway. Everyone hated that – the worry of being found in the ocean by humans, the reality of what could happen if we were locked up on land and kept from the water for too long.

My family knew that all too well.

He nodded as though he'd read my mind. "It hurts, this cost. The penalty we bear for straying from the known path of hiding, of so-called safety. It holds us hostage, not only to our fears for ourselves, but our fears for our loved ones. We live all the time with the dread that a human will discover a way through the magic that protects our cities, or that we will be trapped on land and prevented from returning to the water. We live in fear of our *lives*, and we are taught that this fear is simply 'the way things must be'.

Kirzan's brow rose encouragingly. "Yet, what if I told you it wasn't always like this? And what if I told you that things could change?"

He waited. I said nothing.

"Our people – *your* people – are lost. It pains me to say this, and yet... do you not see it too? What species other than *prey* hides for its life from all others around? What other creature in the ocean – in the *world* – has our power, yet shrinks from creatures weaker than itself? Humans do not. Humans never would. And yet *we* are the ones who have settled into a life of hiding, while they sink deeper and deeper hooks into everything on this Earth. With all our knowledge of the natural order, tell me… how is it possible that this is the way things are meant to be?"

Behind him, several of the other dehaians nodded angrily.

"We've lost sight of the truth," Kirzan continued, "Above the water, we blend to survive the current state of affairs, but beneath the waves we do nothing to change this situation. We accept this reality. We mimic the humans with our games, with our tools, with our very language and behavior, while never acknowledging the truth that is right in front of our eyes.

"We were never meant to be like them. We were meant to rule them."

His folded hands opened in front of him. "Look at the evidence. Our strength. Our speed. Our abilities that far surpass any of their own. If they were meant to have been in charge of this world, they would have the same. They would be designed for it. But they are not.

"And yet we are the ones who hide.

"Some would say we have no choice, that our inability to stray too far from our watery home gives evidence that the land is for them and the ocean for us. And yet, that proves my point precisely. Our people have forgotten their past. They have forgotten what we were once capable of, and the powers we once controlled."

He paused. "But we can change that. Our destiny is our own – more now than it has been for centuries – and through one act, our power can be restored. It seems too simple a solution, yet are not all profound things truly simple at their heart? Our people can be freed. Our children can be made safe. Our homes can be protected. All it takes is one choice.

Kirzan studied me. "Wouldn't you want that?"

My brow twitched down at his words.

"I know who you are, young man. All in this room recognize you. Zekerian Ociras, called Zeke by those closest to him. And we know the stories of your sister, too. The little one, Miri. The one who was lost."

Already pounding, my heart found a way to pick up speed.

He smiled. "We are not monsters, Zeke. We want what is best for our people, just as I know you do. We would do anything for our loved ones, just as I know you would. And when offered the chance to transform the world into a place of safety for everyone we love... any of us would take it."

Kirzan paused. "Will you?"

My jaw clenched as he waited. "What do you want?"

"One gift," he answered. "One creature that has been destined for this purpose since the corrupted act of her creation. And then we can make the world safe for dehaians once more. I confess, we've struggled to find her, since we only spotted her at a distance before the humans rushed her away. For days, we've been hunting any who appeared to be her – bringing them beneath the waves, granting them our special blend of neiphiandine to speed the transformation necessary for the ritual and stifle their ability to cause trouble at the same time – but they have all been human, and so we have been forced to keep searching."

My blood went cold. Human girls. Merciful waves, these psychos had dragged human girls underwater, holding them there with some messed-up version of a dehaian drug in their system until they drowned.

I wanted to be sick.

"But you have changed that," Kirzan continued. "You have confirmed for us which among the humans is actually the girl we seek. And now all that remains is to complete her destiny. To bring her to us. To claim our birthright through her sacrifice, so that none of these lesser beings can threaten us any longer."

I stared. Chloe. They were talking about Chloe.

"You want…" I began.

His expression became pitying. "I understand your confusion. She seems to be an attractive young woman. What man wouldn't find her appealing? But *you* must understand, she is not what you think she is. Her blood is corrupt. She is not dehaian; she is not *anything*. And yet, as all beings do, she has a purpose. One that we can fulfill for her."

Forcibly, I kept my gaze from sliding to the stone table and the chains hanging there.

"You try to be a true son of the dehaian, Zeke. I can see this in you. I know that your heart lies with protecting your people, in protecting those like your little sister, so that nothing like that will ever happen again. And such a future is possible. You have the power in your grasp, young man.

"All you must do is bring her here."

He watched me, his dark eyes scanning my face while behind him, the other dehaians waited.

I couldn't feel my hands anymore. They'd pulled so tight against the shackles that they'd gone numb. And meanwhile, the psychos expected me to agree with Kirzan. To consent to bring Chloe down here so they could do who-knew-what to her, all under some mad belief that this one girl could magically change reality.

Or that her death – her sacrificial, butchered, twisted *death* – could change reality.

I made myself keep breathing. "No."

Kirzan's expression became earnest. "Do not let this creature cloud your judgment, Zeke. Her pretense of ignorance is just that: a pretense. It is only meant to deceive you. She was *intended* for this purpose, destined to spill her blood since before any of us were born. The signs are clear to prove what she is. She changes the water with her presence. She calls to it with her very being, just as the stories said she would. It is so clear. So obvious. And you are not protecting what is right by sparing her; far from it! You are refusing to accept the gift we have been given and deciding that innocent children should die in her place. You are offering their lives for hers, when hers is the one that could save them. Surely, Zeke. *Surely* you wouldn't do this. Offer Miri... for *her?*"

I couldn't keep the rage from my face.

"I don't mean to cause you pain," he implored. "I simply

wish you to understand that you have the power to change this for *all* your people, not just Miri or your siblings who survived. All you have to do is deliver her to us – quickly, while we can still inhibit her ability to fight – and you will save so many from ever suffering as your sister did."

Anger quivered in my chest like a trapped fish, and my muscles were so tense, they trembled. My arms ached with the desire to strike out at him for bringing up Miri over and over again. For trying to manipulate me with her memory. So many people had gone through hell over that, and now this bastard, this psychotic cultic *bastard*, thought he could use that nightmare to make me kill some girl I'd just broken the law to save.

From them.

They'd been the ones who attacked Chloe. I was sure of it, if for no other reason than I didn't believe in *that* level of coincidence. They'd nearly killed her, and definitely killed who knew how many human girls too, and now they wanted me to finish the job.

Because of Miri. Because of the thought of what she must have gone through before the end.

I shivered, pushing the images away.

"Go to hell," I told him.

"Zeke–"

"I said go to hell!"

He fell silent, and from his eyes the earnest light faded, leaving something darker and colder. "She's driven her hooks deep into you, hasn't she? Convinced you of an innocence she cannot truthfully possess?" He paused. "Who would you sacrifice to spare her life, Zeke? Would you offer up Ina, your own twin? Or perhaps your older brothers, Ren and Niall?"

I couldn't breathe. "You stay away from them."

Kirzan smiled. "It is only a question."

He studied me for a moment, and then looked to the other dehaians. "Watch him," he ordered. "Give him some time to think. Perhaps the poison of her influence will fade, once he's reflected for a while."

His gaze flicked back to me and his lips curved again into something too cruel to be a smile. "We will focus our efforts on retrieving her, now that we know where she hides."

Kirzan left the cave, most of the other dehaians following him.

My heart was pounding. My arms pulled at the chains holding me.

It wouldn't take them long to find her. Depending on wherever the hell I was, they might be able to reach Santa Lucina in no time at all.

Or my home in Nyciena.

My muscles quivered. I had to get out of here.

Making myself keep breathing, I turned my focus to the two men guarding me. Both easily outweighed me, and would stand several inches taller than me as well. In their hands, they held net-launchers, same as the kind they'd used to catch me earlier.

The closest one smirked when he saw me studying him.

I looked away, my gaze falling to the shackles of magic-preserved metal encasing the length of my forearms and the chains holding them to the wall. I twitched, pulling at them again.

They didn't budge.

I closed my eyes, rage pounding through me. There had to be a way out of here.

Somehow, there had to be.

∽ 11 ∾

CHLOE

The sun had climbed over the horizon a couple hours ago, and a cloudless blue sky waited beyond the window, promising a beautiful summer day. Past the guest room door, I could hear people moving in the hall, heading for the kitchen and the breakfast I could already smell below.

I'd barely slept. The ocean had been there every time I closed my eyes, sending me gasping back to reality with my hands clutching at my legs in case they'd changed. It hadn't taken long for me to stop lying down, and to sit instead with my back pressed to the headboard and my legs hugged tightly to my chest, while my hands rubbed them intermittently to make sure my skin stayed the same.

It'd made for a long night.

In the other bed, Baylie drew a breath and then rolled over. Her eyes opened, and came to rest on me. Her brow furrowed.

"Morning," she said. "You okay?"

I nodded. "Just couldn't sleep."

Pushing the blankets away, I climbed from the bed.

I could feel her watching me.

"Bad dreams?" she asked.

"Something like that."

I pulled my clothes from my bag. Blankets rustled behind me as she moved to do the same.

"Okay," she allowed. "Well... what do you want to do today?"

Tugging my shirt down over my head, I didn't answer. I didn't know how. Last time I went into town, I'd ended up in the hospital, and the time before that, the boat nearly sank. My track record in Santa Lucina wasn't exactly great, and at the moment, I kind of just wanted to hop into the nearest car and drive away as fast as possible.

Though from what Zeke had said, that might be even harder for me to do now than it had been before.

Feeling nauseated, I drew a steadying breath and focused on tying my hair back in a ponytail. "Whatever you want is fine," I told her.

She was silent for a moment. "Were the dreams about... you know?"

My heart jumped. I looked back at her. "Huh?"

"Jesse."

My panic cleared. Of course she wasn't asking about the ocean. I hadn't told her anything about that and I wasn't going to.

I desperately wanted a car out of here.

"No," I said. "It was… other stuff. Nothing. It's fine."

I tried for a smile.

She didn't look convinced. "You want to talk about it?"

An incredulous laugh bubbled up inside me, though nothing was funny at all. Swallowing it back down, I shook my head. "I'm fine. Really."

I stuffed my pajamas back into the bag and then headed for the door. A moment passed before she followed.

In the kitchen, Diane already had breakfast prepared. Fresh-baked muffins were piled high in a basket next to a glass carafe of orange juice. Bacon slices and eggs took up other plates nearby, all on top of a brightly patterned tablecloth.

I picked up a muffin and a small plate, and then hesitated, my gaze twitching toward the view beyond the dining room table and just as quickly darting away. The sea air drifting through the open windows made shivers run over my skin, and tears wanted to rise at the feeling.

I couldn't be in here.

Turning abruptly, I walked past Baylie, hurrying to the sitting room near the front door.

I could feel her watching me the whole way.

In the front room, I dropped into one of the stiff armchairs that flanked a tiny lamp table. Through the window, I could see the driveway and the gate that led to the road. Bushes lined the perimeter of the property, blocking most of the view of the neighborhood.

Working to calm down, I drew a breath and then took a

bite of the muffin.

I needed to get out of here.

Squeezing my eyes shut, I tried to push the thought away. I didn't have a car, and I couldn't exactly take Baylie's. She sort of needed it to get home. But our 'vacation', or whatever it could be called now, wasn't due to be over for another three days.

And I wasn't sure I could keep from having a breakdown for that long.

My eyes stung. This was so stupid. My whole life, I'd wanted to visit the ocean. But that was *normal*, not because my skin turned to scales and some boy claimed I was part fish. Part *fish*. It was madness.

I mean, sure, I'd been drawn to the water. But really, besides my parents, who wasn't? Baylie loved it here, and Noah had as much as said he felt the same way as me. Plenty of people out there probably did too. Sailors, and oceanographers, and all sorts of people. There wasn't anything weird about that.

It didn't mean everyone was a *fish* thing.

Though I doubted many of them took a bus halfway across the country on some strange compulsion they couldn't shake. A compulsion that made them nearly go out of their minds at the idea of being too far from the water.

I swallowed. When I was a kid, I'd wished I was a mermaid. But I'd wished for a lot of things – among them, to be a bird, a princess, or if nothing else, just to be adopted. But that didn't mean much. Lots of kids daydreamed about those sorts of things.

And fantasizing about swimming through the ocean was a far cry from watching your body change into something else right before your eyes.

Shivering, I looked back to the window. Past the gate, a gray-haired man strolled by, his hands clasped idly behind his back and his gaze drifting over the house as he walked along.

The urge to hide struck me, as though from a hundred yards off, he could see the thing I was inside.

I turned away, tears burning my eyes. It was ridiculous. I was jumpy and I needed distance from this place. From the ocean, and kidnappers, and boys who could talk underwater. But there wasn't anywhere to go.

Except home.

My gaze dropped to the half-eaten muffin on the plate. It was an option. As weird as home could be, it was a strangeness to which I'd long since become accustomed.

And right now, that'd practically be comforting.

Drawing a shaky breath, I rose to take the plate to the kitchen. Mom and Dad probably weren't too far away. And once we were back in Kansas, they could ground me till Armageddon if they wanted. I didn't care.

I just needed to get out of here.

Baylie and Diane watched me as I came into the kitchen. Avoiding their eyes, I made a beeline for the counter and put the plate in the sink. Neither of them spoke as I left again, though it seemed like I'd interrupted them talking.

And vain as it felt to think it, something in the way they looked made it seem like the conversation had been about me.

Up in the guest room, I shut the door behind me and crossed to the nightstand. Grabbing my cell, I dialed Dad's number and then waited as the line rang.

No answer.

My brow furrowed as the voicemail clicked on. I considered leaving a message, but hung up and then dialed Mom instead.

Seconds slid past. The phone kept ringing. I glanced to the door, wondering if anyone else had heard from them since their message a few days ago.

"Hello?"

My attention snapped back. "Mom?"

"Chloe?"

"Yeah. Look, I was wondering–"

"How are you?"

I paused. It sounded like an accusation, not a question.

"I-I'm okay," I lied. "I just–"

"Are you sure?"

My brow drew down. "Mom, what is it? Why are you–"

"Have you gone back in the water, Chloe?"

I tensed at her harsh tone, feeling suddenly like I was five years old again. "No."

Which was technically true. Sort of, anyway.

She let out a breath on the other end of the line. "Good. Don't. Just… we're on our way. We'll be there as soon as we can."

"Where are you?"

She hesitated. "Your father had a minor health issue. But he's fine. The doctors—"

"Doctors? What happened?"

"It's fine."

"Mom!"

The pause came again, like out of a million responses, she was cherry picking only certain ones.

"Your father had a very minor problem that required a doctor's attention. But we'll be on the road again as soon as he's cleared to leave the hospital, which should be this afternoon."

I was speechless. Swallowing hard, I tried to regroup. "Wh-what was wrong?"

"It's not your concern."

I looked down, the phone still clutched to my ear. He'd really looked bad when I left.

"Is he going to be okay?"

She was silent for a moment. "We just need to get home and everything will be fine."

Guilt chewed at me. I'd run off, and then this happened. But if I hadn't, maybe…

"Mom, why are you guys so crazy about the ocean? I mean, is there something—"

"We are *not* crazy, Chloe."

I grimaced. They were, but whatever. I didn't want to

argue. And I had no idea how to ask what I needed to know. Was it because I was a fish creature? A de-whatever or mermaid? And for that matter, were they?

How was I supposed to say that?

"Is there a reason, Mom?"

A heartbeat passed. "It's dangerous. There are... sharks. Diseases."

I let out a groan. *She* didn't even sound like she believed the words.

"Mom, what the hell is it?"

"Don't you swear at me, young lady."

"I'm serious! I... something happened, okay? I met this guy and he—"

"What guy?"

I hesitated. "Just a guy. But he said some stuff. About me. About the, uh..."

"Chloe, you listen to me. You stay away from him. We'll be there soon."

"Mom, *please*! Why are you so scared about the ocean? And don't say it's because of diseases. I... I know that's not it."

I waited, barely breathing, and for the longest time, she was silent.

"Mom?"

"We'll talk about this once we get there," she said quietly.

"Mom! Please, I need to know if—"

"I said we'll talk about it once we're there! You stay out of the water, stay away from that boy, and wait for us, do you understand?"

"But I–"

"I mean it, Chloe."

She hung up. My hand shook as I lowered the phone and stared at the screen.

I felt like crying. She never listened. Never. I had no idea when they were going to be here, and if they weren't leaving whatever hospital Dad was staying at until this afternoon...

A breath pressed from my chest as my heart began to pound. I had to get out of here. I didn't want to be this thing. I wanted to be normal. To have normal parents and normal vacations and normal everything and I just–

My arms hurt. I looked down.

A shriek escaped me.

Things were emerging from the backs of my forearms. In a single row from my wrists to my elbows and pointing away from my hands, spikes like translucent, iridescent knives pushed bloodlessly through my skin. With every second, they grew longer, gradually beginning to fan outward.

"No, no," I begged, choking on a sob. Shaking hard, my fingers tried to push them down, but they were so sharp, they pricked my fingertips. I could feel the pressure of the contact beneath my skin, though, as if the spikes were attached to the muscle and bone there. "Stop. Oh God, please stop."

A knock at the door made me jump. Frantic, I looked around, trying to find some way to hide my arms.

"Chloe?"

Baylie opened the door. Desperately, I dropped the phone and tucked my arms behind my back.

"Yeah?" I said.

She paused. "You okay?"

"Fine."

Her brow drew down. "Well, um… we were thinking of doing a movie day. Maybe just hanging out here, taking it easy for a while. That sound good to you?"

I couldn't think of anything worse, short of going to the beach. Not right now.

But I couldn't say that. And I really needed her to leave. "Sure."

Her concerned expression didn't fade. "You sure you're okay?"

"Uh-huh."

"Alright, well, we'll be downstairs whenever you want to join us."

I nodded.

She hesitated a moment more, and then left the room, pulling the door closed behind her.

I let out a breath. Trembling, I brought my arms back into view.

The spikes were gone. Nothing but my own skin remained, without a single trace that anything had been pushing through it only moments ago.

Tears stung my eyes. I had to get out of here. I had to find some way to stop this, before something else impossible and horrible came along.

And before anyone found out what was happening to me.

We watched movies till after dark.

And I barely remembered a single one.

It hadn't taken me long to ask the others if they wouldn't mind closing the windows of the living room. The sea air made me tremble. My hands twitched to rub my legs or arms every few seconds, and by the time the movies were over, I was a cramped ball of muscle from trying to hold still.

But thankfully, nothing else weird had happened to my body, and when I stood to help the others bring the popcorn bowls back to the kitchen, my relief at that simple fact left me shaking. Diane set to washing the bowls in the sink and Baylie grabbed a towel. Fighting to keep my gaze from being pulled toward the ocean, I took the dried dishes and returned them to the cupboards.

While hoping every second to hear the sound of my parents' car pulling into the driveway.

Finally, the last dish was put away. Baylie hung the towels up to dry as Maddox and Noah called goodnight and headed to their rooms. Peter had gone upstairs a few minutes before, and without anything else to do, I returned to the living room to collect the blanket I'd been curled under for the past few films.

I jumped as Diane touched my arm.

"You doing okay, honey?" she asked quietly.

"Y-yeah. I'm fine."

Her mouth tightened. "Chloe, you've been on edge since this morning. More than I've seen you since that horrible man attacked. Now, I know this isn't quite the same as the hospital, but... has something happened? Is there some other reason you're so tense?"

She looked up at me, her brown eyes so earnest, I didn't know what to say. I couldn't hope to tell anyone here what was happening, and as much as I'd tried to hide it, the others obviously had picked up on how anxious I'd been. But the only option I could see for fixing this – and for staying *human* – was to get out of here as quickly as possible. How did I explain that?

Struggling to find words, I turned away, my gaze landing on the view beyond the living room windows.

A man stood by the bushes at the edge of the lawn.

I gasped.

"What is it?" Diane asked.

The man stepped back through the bushes and disappeared.

"Chloe?"

"A man." I pointed. "There. He was right there, watching the house. He–"

"Peter!" Diane called.

I stared at the place where the man had been standing while footsteps pounded on the stairs.

"What?" Peter said, coming into the kitchen.

"Chloe saw someone outside."

"Where?"

I pointed again. "The bushes. Watching the house."

Peter nodded. He opened a drawer and drew out a flashlight. "You all just stay put."

He headed out the door. Baylie retreated across the kitchen toward us while, at my side, I could see Diane wringing her hands. Silent, we watched him approach the edge of the yard.

The beam of the flashlight swept the bushes. A minute ticked past, and then he turned, coming back to the house.

"He's gone, whoever he was," Peter said. He tucked the flashlight back into the drawer. "I'll call the police though. Ask them to do a patrol of the area, just in case."

Diane nodded. Taking my arm, she steered me toward the hall. "You girls go on upstairs, okay? The police will take care of this."

She gave Baylie a pointed look.

Baylie nodded. "Yeah. Okay." She motioned for me to go ahead of her.

Feeling shepherded, I fought the urge to look back at the window as I left the room.

Noah opened the door to his bedroom as we came up the stairs.

"Everything okay?" he asked.

"Chloe saw someone outside," Baylie said. "He got away, but Peter's calling the police."

Noah looked to me and from the way his concerned gaze checked me over, I suddenly felt like he could see straight through me to the spikes and scales and God knew what else.

"You guys alright?" he asked.

I didn't answer.

Baylie nodded. "Just going to try to go to bed."

"Okay…"

He was still watching me. I turned away, heading for the guest room.

"Let me know if you need anything," he finished, sounding confused.

"Yeah, okay." Baylie replied. "Thanks."

I kept walking, and pushed the door closed behind me as I reached the bedroom. Taking my cell from my pocket, I thumbed on the phone and checked for messages for the thousandth time. I'd had it in my pocket all day, just in case. But still, there was nothing.

Behind me, I heard Baylie come into the room and shut the door.

"Chloe," she said flatly.

I didn't turn around.

Making a furious noise, she strode across the room and grabbed my arm, pulling me around. "What's going on? Seriously, I'm sick of this. Talk to me."

I tugged my arm from her grip and tucked it behind my back for fear of it growing spikes in her hand. Shaking my head, I looked away. "Everything's fine."

She scoffed. "Yeah, right. You look like you're about ready to climb out of your skin."

An incredulous laugh threatened to emerge. I choked it back down.

"What's *wrong?*"

I shivered, my gaze rising to the view through the bedroom window. I couldn't explain to anyone here. What was I supposed to say? I'm a de-thing mermaid creature with knife-like spikes on my arms?

They'd think I was nuts.

"Chloe, please. What is it?"

I looked down, trying not to wince at her imploring tone. I *wanted* to tell her, though. Dear God, I wanted to tell her. I'd known Baylie since we were four. She was as close to me as a sister and we'd told each other everything for years. But this...

A pained expression twisted my face. If anybody would understand, and not think I was a monster or a lunatic...

Biting my lip, I turned back toward her. "Okay, look. I–"

Glass shattered downstairs. Someone gave a shout, and then there was a crashing sound.

For a moment, we were both paralyzed, and then Baylie spun and yanked open the door. I raced after her down the hall.

Noah rushed from his bedroom.

"What the hell?" Maddox cried, throwing open his own door.

Not answering, we ran down the stairs.

The front door stood open and the window of the sitting room was shattered. Somebody was making a dash for the end of the driveway, while Peter stood in the middle of the room with Diane in the hall behind him. On the floor, a man lay below the wreckage of a china cabinet.

I gaped.

Maddox started out the door to catch the figure fleeing toward the street.

"Stay put!" Peter ordered, barely taking his eyes from the unconscious man. "Noah, call the police."

Noah raced toward the kitchen phone.

"What happened?" Maddox demanded.

"Intruder," Peter responded. He twitched his head toward the open door. "Get that closed."

Maddox did as he said.

"Girls, go back upstairs," Peter continued. "You don't need to be down here for this."

"But who–" Baylie started.

He looked over at her.

She swallowed and nodded. Reaching out, she took my arm, pulling me with her.

I couldn't take my eyes from the intruder. He was dressed in a black, hooded jacket and dark pants, and he looked like he'd been thrown straight into the glass display case. Blood dripped from a gash on his head and his arm was twisted awkwardly beneath him. In steady rhythm, though, his chest rose and fell, giving evidence that he was still alive.

Baylie tugged my arm harder. I trailed her from the room.

Sirens howled in the distance as we climbed the stairs. Baylie slowed when we neared the top of the steps and without speaking, we both stopped at the landing to watch the first floor.

The police arrived. A detective pulled Peter aside to talk to him, while several officers strode into the other room to retrieve the intruder.

Diane caught sight of us. "Girls," she said, hurrying up the steps toward us. "Peter told you to get to bed."

A chagrinned expression crossed Baylie's face. "Sorry. We just—"

Diane cut her off with a shushing gesture. "I know, but the police are handling this. You don't need to worry."

I hesitated as Baylie walked back along the hall. Over Diane's head, I looked down at the first floor. The officers emerged from the sitting room, the man between them. He'd woken up at some point, though he still seemed dazed. Handcuffs trapped his wrists, and as the police led him from the room, his gaze swept the area as if he was searching for something.

And then he spotted me.

Hatred consumed his confusion.

"Abomination!" he yelled. He lurched in the officers' grip, trying to throw them off. "Filthy spawn of a landwalker whore!"

He thrashed, hurling an officer to the ground. The cops shouted, and several more of their number rushed over to help hold the suspect who'd suddenly gone berserk.

"You'll never hide from us all!" He stumbled beneath the weight of the cops wrestling him down. "You're dead, you hear me? You and the creatures protecting you! *Dead!*"

The police hauled him toward the door. He twisted in their grasp, his gaze finding me again.

And for a heartbeat, his eyes glowed.

The cops dragged him from the house. Peter slammed the door after them.

I couldn't move.

"What the *hell*..." I heard Baylie say behind me.

Peter paused, one hand to the door, and then he looked to Diane. On some unspoken signal, the woman nodded and then turned, reaching up to take my hand.

I jumped, air entering my lungs for the first time in a small eternity, and the skin of my forearms stung.

Panic raced through me. Tugging my hand away, I tucked my arms behind my back.

Diane's brow furrowed in confusion.

I was shaking too hard to form the words I needed to apologize. Looking between her and Baylie, I retreated around them both, keeping my back to the wall and my arms as out of sight as I could.

"Chloe, it's okay," Diane said, coming up the stairs after me. "You're safe. He was just a crazy person. The cops have him now."

Baylie stared at me as I moved past her and continued down the hallway.

"You're *okay*," Diane assured me. "Honey, I promise. You're safe."

I sped up, turning and breaking into a run as the corner blocked me from their view. Hurrying into the guest room, I grabbed at the door and shut it as fast as I could.

Trembling, I lifted my arms. The spikes were retracting into my skin.

A sob choked me.

I wanted to go home. For the first time in my life, I wanted to be home more than anything in the world.

The spikes disappeared. My skin sealed over the spaces where they'd been, leaving no trace.

I closed my eyes.

"Chloe?" Baylie called from the other side of the door.

I tensed. Beyond the wood of the door, I could hear people talking, their voices too low to understand.

Seconds slid past.

"Chloe?" Baylie tried again. "We don't have to stay here, okay? Peter and Diane are—"

She cut off as I yanked open the door.

"What'd you say?" I asked.

She blinked, taken back. "Uh, we don't have to stay. They don't want to, I mean. Everybody's pretty freaked out, so Peter wants to call your parents, tell them where we're going, and then just board up the window and spend a few days at the family cabin till things get fixed up."

I stared at her. "Where?"

"About an hour or so from here."

"A-away from the ocean?" I struggled to get the words out.

Her brow furrowed as she nodded. "In the mountains."

A breath escaped me. "When?"

"Soon. We only need to–"

I was already heading for my bag.

"Are you alright?" Baylie asked as she followed me into the room. "I mean, not alright, but…"

I couldn't answer. I just needed to get out of here before the horrible compulsion to stay caught me and made it impossible to leave.

At my silence, Baylie sighed. I glanced back to see her heading for her own things.

"You can talk to me, you know," she said without taking her eyes from her luggage. "I'm just saying."

I swallowed. "It's… complicated."

"How?" she demanded, looking back at me. "*How* is it complicated? Did you know that guy or something?"

"No. I just…" My fingers rubbed at my forearm. "A lot's happened this week."

She waited. From the first floor, the sound of hammering rose.

"You ever feel like you're losing your mind?" I whispered.

She paused. "How so?" she asked cautiously.

"Like there are things happening to you that you can't control? That you don't want... but they won't stop?"

"Chloe, you're scaring me. What's going on?"

"It's just... you remember what happened with the boat? Well, when I fell over, there was this guy. In the water. And, um, I could hear him... like, talking to me and—"

I cut off as Diane came around the corner.

"You girls ready?"

I looked to Baylie uncomfortably.

Baylie sighed. "Yeah."

Diane headed for the stairs. Baylie picked up her bag and followed, pausing as she passed me.

"Lots of people see things when they're in trouble, Chloe," she said quietly. "It doesn't mean you're losing your mind, okay?"

I closed my eyes as she left the room. I wanted to tell her. To explain. And maybe I could, just as soon as we reached the cabin and were somewhere the others couldn't hear.

Fishhooks started to bite into my skin. Gasping, I hefted my bag and rushed for the stairs, trying to stay ahead of the feeling.

❧ 12 ❧

ZEKE

Hours had passed and every one of them had been too long. The guards had changed in shifts, watching me and smirking and holding onto their weapons without ever coming close enough for me to do anything about the situation. Kirzan hadn't returned, and neither had most of the others who'd gone with him, though the men who'd stayed looked more and more satisfied with every shift.

And it was really hard not to worry about what that might mean.

In all the hours I'd been here, I'd argued with myself over what to do if I got free. I could go after Chloe and warn her about the freaks who were hunting her, or I could go to Nyciena.

Because everyone needed to know these psychos were still around.

And because fact was, I'd need help to keep the dozens of Sylphaen from doing whatever the hell it was they planned

158

for her. Yet, just like the last time the bastards had tried to catch her, it was entirely possible they'd do something terrible to her before I even got out of here, let alone returned all the way from Nyciena.

And so I chased myself in circles, knowing that the only solution lay in finding the nearest communication relay station, getting in touch with Dad, and then doing what I could to help her while hoping Ina, Niall, and Ren stayed safe.

Even if breaking free was looking less and less likely with every goliath dehaian Kirzan sent to guard me.

I grimaced, watching the stone-faced guards. With military precision, they'd kept their distance, giving me no chance of grabbing them or somehow getting the key from their hands. Every attempt I'd made to goad them closer had been met with silence as well, and in the past half-hour, I'd nearly given up.

A pained curse came from the tunnel, and then two dehaians swam into the cave, one of them rubbing his arm and tossing a glare over his shoulder at the rock walls.

My eyebrow twitched up. Unlike the pair of men watching me now, these two were younger. Smaller. Maybe five years older than me, or my brother Ren's age at most. One had a mop of brown hair, curly even under the water, and the other was pale enough that his blond hair blended with his skin and his watery eyes barely showed up on his pasty face. The other guards looked incredulous and disgusted in turn at the sight of them both, and one scoffed.

"Wisdom Kirzan sent *you?*"

The brown-haired guy's expression turned surly. "Yeah, well, it got complicated. He asked us to do this while you and the rest go to Plan B."

"*Asked* you," the man sneered. "Right. Just don't screw this up too, eh?"

Barely concealed fury twitched across the mop-headed guy's face at the words, but he didn't respond.

The man laughed and handed the blond guy the key to my shackles. Together, he and the other guard left the cave.

My brow drew down. The curly-haired guy turned back, catching sight of my expression.

"What?" he spat.

I paused. He was already angry. If I could rile him up enough to get him to come closer, maybe I could grab him and make his buddy unlock these restraints.

"What'd you do?" I asked.

"Shut up."

I ignored him. "That bad? What, you forget to bring Kirzan his dinner or something?" I scoffed. "You all obviously aren't the top of the pecking order around here, so…"

"He said shut up," the pale guy snapped. He glanced to his buddy. "Ignore this scum. He's not worth it."

"Obviously I'm worth it enough for you two reschiatas to be assigned here rather than out on the real mission," I chuckled, throwing in an Yvarian insult for good measure. "And your buddies barely seem to think *you're* worth doing this."

The brown-haired guy's face twisted with rage at my words, and he swam closer. I braced my hands on the wall, getting ready to grab him.

"You want to know what I did?" he growled. "I bashed that bitch's head in. I would've gotten her bloody little body here too, if her stupid friend hadn't managed a good shot with some pepper spray."

My amused look couldn't sustain, overwhelmed as it was by the memory of what Chloe had looked like in the hospital.

"You were the one who did that?" I asked, my voice going cold as I realized who this was. Jesse. The guy Chloe had mentioned. The one from the bookstore.

He smirked.

My heart was pounding. "You nearly killed her."

"Wait till you see what we do to her later," Jesse sneered. "A little of our special neiphiandine, a few knives..."

I could feel myself shaking and it took everything I had to push the rage down and make myself keep breathing. Stay focused. Not imagine what I could do if he came just a *bit* closer.

"Is that right?" I commented quietly. "Well, aren't you the big man when you're faced with *one* girl? One girl you couldn't even catch." I looked him over, my disgust anything but feigned. "No wonder they think you're so pathetic."

Jesse's nostrils flared. "I could show you pathetic," he warned, tapping the net-launcher against his palm.

I scoffed.

His doughy face turning red, Jesse swam toward me. "Now you listen to me, you cocky little—"

He came within reach. Twisting in the shackles, I lunged upward and wrapped my tail around his head.

His weapon rising, the blond guy started forward, his eyes wide.

"Don't," I warned, squeezing in on Jesse's head. In my grip, he thrashed, unable to breathe, and his fists pummeled at my scales. I gritted my teeth, hanging on. "You shoot that thing at me, he's dead, understand?"

The blond guy hesitated.

"You want to explain to Kirzan how your buddy died?" I snapped, tightening my hold as Jesse kicked and twisted. "Drop the weapon and unlock these damn restraints!"

For another moment, the guy didn't move. His gaze darted between me and Jesse.

I could feel Jesse getting weaker. His fists still punched me, though the blows were half as strong as before.

And on some level, I found I couldn't quite care.

The pale guy let the weapon fall as he rushed forward. His fingers fumbled with the lock, and then the shackles dropped from my hands.

I shoved away from the wall and flung Jesse aside, sending him tumbling into the pit at the center of the cave as I took off for the exit.

Pods of nets shot past me, splattering against the wall, and

I could hear Jesse shouting choked curses as he scrambled from the pit. Kicking hard for extra speed, I darted into the tunnel. Rock surrounded me, twisting and turning with shadows and infrequent light. I swore, racing as fast as I could for an exit that never seemed to arrive.

Jesse's shouts echoed through the tunnel as he tried to chase after me.

I sped around a corner, and the endless rock opened up into blue water. Letting out a breath of relief, I cast a swift look around and then left the tunnel behind, swimming like hell for a relay station where I could warn everyone that these bastards were back again.

13

CHLOE

It was long after midnight by the time we reached the cabin.

"Okay," Diane said as she pulled the sedan to a stop. "Well, here we are."

I looked out the window. The darkness was thick and, shadowed from the moonlight by the trees, the cabin was hard to see. Logs formed the walls, and the entire building looked vaguely like a two-story triangle with a porch attached. The Delaneys rented the house to tourists most of the year, but for this week, it was empty.

Diane pushed open the car door while, up ahead, Maddox and Noah climbed from the other sedan with their father.

"The cleaning crew should have put blankets on the beds," Diane continued while we got out, "but if they didn't, everything's in the closet. The sleeper couch is broken, though – we were going to have a new one delivered this week – so you'll have to share the upstairs room with the boys. I hope that's okay?"

She glanced back to us. One hand on Daisy's collar and the other stifling a yawn, Baylie nodded. I just swallowed uncomfortably, and then trailed them both to the door.

The smell of pine surrounded us as we came inside, and as Peter turned on the light, I could see that wood made up a good portion of the décor. A carved mantle hung over the fireplace in one corner of the living room, and the furniture was all framed by polished wood as well. A cathedral ceiling rose above the front room, and the landing of the stairs on the second floor overlooked the space.

"Okay, well," Diane said, "the bathrooms are by your room and then just past the stairs down here, and Peter and I will be in there," she nodded toward a door on the opposite side of the living room, "so just let us know if you need anything, alright?"

She smiled, though it seemed a bit forced. "Everything's going to be fine. You'll see."

I tried to smile in return, failed miserably, and then followed Baylie upstairs.

In the second floor bedroom, Noah and Maddox had already set their bags by the bunk bed near the door. Baylie glanced to me questioningly, and when I shrugged, she crossed to the other side of the room and tossed her bag up to the top bunk there.

I hesitated, and then took my backpack into the bathroom to get changed.

The guys were in bed by the time I returned. While Baylie headed to the bathroom to put on her pajamas, I slid beneath the blankets, grateful that they didn't feel too scratchy against my skin. I seemed to be doing okay thus far, even at this distance from the ocean, though I was still so tense my muscles ached. But I hadn't felt like running out the door or stealing the car or anything, which I counted as a minor victory, given how things had gone the last time I left town.

Baylie came back and flipped off the light switch by the door. The bunk bed creaked as she climbed the wooden ladder and then got under the blankets. Pulling the floral-patterned quilt up to my chin, I shifted around on the soft mattress and then closed my eyes as silence fell over the room.

The ocean was waiting.

I tensed as the water enveloped me. I didn't want to be there, but unlike the night before, I couldn't snap myself back to consciousness. I was too tired, and the pull of the water was too strong.

Shivers ran through me as the current carried me along. It was warm, more comforting than anything at that depth should have been, and seemed to sink into me, giving me energy. I could feel my skin try to change in response, and I gasped, fighting to hang onto who and what I was.

Ice twisted across my spine.

Gasping, I spun. Blue twilight surrounded me for as far as my eyes could see, but suddenly, in the distance, darkness began to take hold. Like a black cloud, it spread through the water, sending the temperature plummeting and consuming all the light.

And coming for me.

I could feel it, though I didn't know why. The blackness was coming for me. Chasing me. It wanted something and without question, I knew that something wasn't good. Fear gripped my chest and I kicked hard, trying to swim away.

But it was faster.

Darkness engulfed me, and in the black, I heard a voice laughing. Coldness crept over me, paralyzing my muscles and making it hard to breathe. I choked, my strength draining as the light vanished completely and something grabbed my shoulders, trapping me and refusing to let go.

"Chloe!"

I screamed, lunging up into a tangle of blankets and Noah's hands on my arms. Radioactive daylight cast the room in vivid relief for a heartbeat and then vanished, plunging everything into darkness.

Maddox swatted the switch on the wall. I cringed at the sudden light.

"What happened?" Baylie cried, leaning over the edge of the top bunk.

Blinking hard, I looked over to see Noah staring at me.

"Nightmare," he answered, as though finding the word on autopilot. "Just a nightmare."

"Chloe?" Baylie asked. "You okay?"

Trembling, I felt my forearms, and breathed again at the

realization they were normal. I nodded. "Y-yeah."

Noah wouldn't stop staring at me. Carefully, he eased away from the bed and then rose to his feet.

The light on the landing came on. "Everything alright?" Diane called from the stairs.

"Yeah, everything's fine," Maddox replied.

A moment passed. The light beyond the door disappeared. His brow drawing down, Noah hesitated and then walked back to his bunk.

Maddox turned off the bedroom light.

I shivered. Noah looked stunned, and I couldn't think of many reasons why. The room had changed when I first woke up. I'd seen everything so brightly, even if only for a second, and I knew what Zeke and those others did with their eyes.

And Noah had been there, watching me...

My hands rubbed at my forearms again.

Across the room, the bunk ladder creaked as Maddox climbed back up, and I could hear the blankets rustle as Noah returned to his bed.

He'd seen something. I was certain of it.

And I had no idea what he was going to do now.

In the darkness, I pulled the blanket up higher, bundling it around me against the cold I could still feel on my skin. I'd thought I'd been doing okay this far from the ocean. I'd hoped maybe things would be alright.

Clearly, I'd been wrong.

$\backsim$ 14 $\backsim$

ZEKE

"No, damn you, I said Sylphaen! The *Sylphaen!*"

I slammed my fist into the boulder as the image of the guard on the other end of the connection wavered. Within the hollow in the stone, the shimmering surface of the relay connection steadied again.

"Did you say Sylphaen?" the guard asked.

"Yes!"

He blinked. Ripples distorted his image as he turned away, saying something I couldn't hear.

"That's not possible," he argued as he looked back to me. "There's no... back... you–"

I let out a furious groan as the guard vanished and the glowing blue-white collection of magic dissipated from the hollow in the boulder. It'd taken me forever to get that damn connection working, and that was after I'd swum for nearly an hour, avoiding outlaws and mercenaries and who knew what else that lived out here, before finally spotting the marker

169

leading to this relay station in the middle of nowhere.

Exhaling, I scowled and pressed my hand to the boulder again, trying to reactivate the magic inside the stone and reclaim the link to the outpost on the edge of Yvaria – the only place I'd been able to reach. Light shivered through the lines beneath the sand, and slowly, the blue-white glow began to accumulate in the hollow again.

"Zeke?" came a scratchy voice from the other end.

The picture solidified.

I blinked, torn between surprise and the urge to swear. "Ren? What are you doing in–"

My oldest brother made an impatient gesture. "No time. You said people claiming to be the Sylphaen attacked you?"

"Yeah."

The connection went scratchy.

"Ren?"

"–come back home, understand?"

I hit the boulder again.

"Zeke?"

"I'm here. What'd you say?"

"I said come back home. Leave whatever you're doing and get home. Let us investigate these–"

"Ren, they're after a dehaian girl in Santa Lucina. They want to kill her."

For a moment, Ren was silent, muscles jumping along the hard line of his jaw. The image wavered and then solidified again.

"–doesn't matter. So just get back here. I'll send people to check on this girl. But you head for Nyciena."

I looked away. Ren lived and breathed responsibility – and that was putting it politely – but he wasn't thinking. I couldn't just go back to Nyciena and let someone else handle it. I was the only one who'd seen Chloe.

Turning back to the relay, I shook my head. "Can't. I'm the only one who knows what she looks like. Just send the guards to Santa Lucina. I'll meet them."

"Zeke, no. This girl isn't–"

"No time, Ren. See you when I get back."

I broke the connection and shoved away from the boulder, taking off into the open water again. I was more than a few hours from Santa Lucina, if the marker I'd found earlier was any indication. But the guards would take awhile to get there as well, and I was pretty sure of the route they'd take. I'd catch them on the way.

Building up speed in the water, I swam for the California coast.

↶ 15 ↷

CHLOE

The others were still in bed when I finally decided to get up. I hadn't slept since my dream the night before, and as the sun crept over the horizon, I concluded it was time to give up the charade and surrender to another night without sleep.

Not that I wanted it. Not if that nightmare was waiting for me.

Shifting my shoulders against the cold still clinging to me, I pulled open the bedroom door and slipped into the hall with my clothes bundled beneath my arm. I changed in the bathroom and folded my pajamas, leaving them in a small pile by the door for lack of anything else to do. I didn't want to wake anyone by heading back into the bedroom.

The first floor was still, and Peter and Diane's door was closed. My stomach growled, the sound loud in the silence, and wincing, I made my way to the kitchen. I'd been too nervous to eat much of anything yesterday, and my body seemed finally ready for me to make up the difference.

Thankfully, Diane had brought food in a cooler when we came up here. I grabbed the milk and cereal, and then hunted through the cabinets for a bowl. Breakfast made, I returned to the living room and sank onto the couch.

Sunlight spread through the room as I ate, the golden beams filtering past the windows that stretched up the height of the wall, all the way to the pinnacle of the room's cathedral ceiling. Setting my empty bowl aside, I pulled my legs up and then hugged them to my chest as I watched the pink and blue morning.

The steps creaked.

I turned. At the top of the stairs, Noah paused. For a moment, he studied me, almost as if deciding what to do, and then slowly, he walked down to the living room.

"Morning."

I swallowed nervously. "Hey."

He glanced to his parents' bedroom, and then came over to the couch. "Sleep okay?" he asked me as he sat down.

I shrugged a shoulder, watching him. He appeared cautious, as if he was picking his words and actions like they were patches of land in a minefield, but he didn't looked nearly as freaked out as I'd expected.

Which was odd.

"You?" I asked warily.

He nodded, his gaze on his hands.

A moment crept by.

"So," he said. "First visit to the ocean."

My brow drew down. It almost seemed like there was a question in the statement.

He glanced up at me and I nodded. Echoing the motion, he dropped his gaze to his hands again. "Quite a trip then, I guess."

I didn't know how to respond.

He drew a breath. "When I was little, my grandfather used to tell me stories. History, he called it. But they were stories of people who weren't quite like everyone else. People who had... abilities." He looked up at me again. "Abilities like making their eyes glow in the dark."

I trembled.

"They loved the ocean, my grandfather said. So much that they couldn't be apart from it. And if they tried... it'd draw them back. It was their home, you see. They couldn't really leave it."

Noah paused. "He called them dehaians."

My arms tightened around my knees, and then I flinched as my skin started to sting. Panicked, I moved to tuck my arms behind my legs.

Noah reached out, his fingers coming to rest on my wrist.

I froze.

"It's alright," he said.

The spikes crept from my forearms. He watched them, not moving away.

"Who are you?" I whispered.

Noah's gaze dropped briefly. "A guy whose grandfather told

him a lot of stories."

"But why…" I tried, trembling as the spikes grew longer. "Why aren't you…"

His mouth tightened and he seemed to struggle through the minefield again, finding the words. "Because sometimes the stories are real, and that's okay."

My brow furrowed.

"Just take a breath," Noah told me. "He said… he said those were your defenses. Some of them. And if you calm down, I bet they'll go away."

I hesitated, and then pulled in a shaky breath. The spikes started to retreat.

"You're safe here, Chloe. I…" He nodded, almost as if to himself. "I promise."

The spikes disappeared into my arms. He took his hand from my wrist.

"You doing okay this far from the ocean?" he asked.

For a moment, I stared at him, shaken by the reality that someone knew the truth and was fine. Not freaking. Not pressuring me to go into the water.

Just treating me like I was normal, and being fine.

"It's not so bad here," I whispered.

A smile flickered across his face and he nodded. "Good."

The bedroom door upstairs opened. Carrying her clothes, Baylie started toward the bathroom and then spotted us.

"Hey there." She paused. "Everything alright?"

I nodded. "Yeah," I replied, feeling like for the first time in a while, the answer was mostly true.

She looked between us. "Okay," she allowed, appearing a bit unconvinced. Eyeing us uncertainly, she walked into the bathroom.

Noah watched her go, and then glanced back to me. "So," he said, his voice low. "If you're doing good here, then you want to do something like people on a regular vacation would? Go hiking, maybe?"

I gave a small laugh, the sound lost somewhere between relief and incredulity. "That'd be nice."

He grinned. "Alright, then," he said, humor in his green eyes. "A regular vacation it is."

"So when do you guys want to take a break?" Baylie called as we headed up the next slope of the trail.

I looked back. The narrow dirt track stretched behind us, twisting in a slow decline down the hillside. Trees sheltered part of the path, and the sunlight cast dark shadows from their branches. At Baylie's heels, Daisy kept pace, panting in the heat of the bright summer day.

"There's a nice stretch of the river up ahead," Maddox offered, hefting the cooler bag higher on his shoulder. "We could do lunch there?"

"Yeah, okay," Baylie agreed.

I kept walking. She sounded tired and hungry, and really, I

should have been as well. I'd barely slept last night and we'd been hiking for the better part of three hours, winding our way through the trails near the Delaneys' cabin. But something about the fresh air and brilliant blue sky just felt so wonderful, I couldn't help but keep moving.

Noah glanced back at me as he crested the slope ahead. I blushed and looked away, my heart picking up speed.

And then there was that.

A smile pulled at my mouth as he continued on. I hadn't expected it to feel this great, having him know what was going on. He was so calm about the whole thing, so *normal*. It was unbelievable, and more than a little exhilarating.

Even if I worried it couldn't last.

Biting my lip, I climbed over the top of the hill and continued down the slope to the next turn of the trail. I didn't *think* he'd told his brother or parents anything, and from the way Maddox was acting, it really seemed like Noah hadn't. But I wasn't certain I could ask him to stay quiet on the subject. In my family, it wouldn't have been a big deal for me to keep things from my mom and dad. I spent most of my time doing that anyway.

But it didn't take a genius to see that the Delaneys were different. Closer than my family had ever been.

I just wasn't sure how I felt about anyone else knowing what was going on.

The trail led around a curve and then opened onto a flat stretch of riverbank. As Daisy ran ahead of us to the water, I followed the guys to the shade of the trees, where Maddox was opening the cooler bag while Noah spread out a picnic blanket.

"So," Baylie said as Maddox fished the food from the bag, "how's college going?"

Maddox handed us both sandwiches. "Not bad. My psych TA from this past semester was a real nutcase, though."

"Well, there's some irony," Baylie observed.

"Yeah, no kidding. He kept insisting we study nine hours a day because, you know, we were in college now, so we needed to suck it up or whatever."

"Seriously? What, was this a class for grads or something?"

He shook his head. "Just a one-hundred level. I was only taking it because I needed the gen-ed credit."

"Oh, good grief."

"I think he believed it was his mission to toughen us up for college or something. Weed out people who, I don't know, he thought were there for the wrong reasons."

"Like getting a gen-ed credit."

"Apparently."

I looked at the river as they kept talking. The water here didn't have the same pull on me as the ocean – maybe because it was freshwater rather than salt. But the current was beautiful as it swept around the rocks, and the sound of the river provided a background to everything the others were saying.

"So'd you stay in the class?" Baylie asked.

"Yeah. Somebody complained to the department head, and

he talked to the guy. Made him calm down a bit."

"Wow. The other TAs aren't like that though, right?"

I kept eating, half-listening as the conversation continued. Maddox had started at USC about two years prior, and Baylie fully intended to go there as well. I did too, for that matter, if only to stay close to her and get near the ocean at the same time.

Though now that I thought about it, I wondered if college would even be a possibility for me.

The others finished their lunch, and Maddox rose to rinse the cooler bag out in the river. Still talking to him, Baylie stood and followed, calling Daisy back toward her as she went.

"You doing alright?" Noah asked as they walked off.

I nodded. "Just wondering about college."

He hesitated. "Where are you planning on going?"

I glanced to him. His face was so carefully neutral, it made my heart pound. "USC. Or, you know, somewhere like that. If I get in, anyway."

"Huh," he commented.

Silence fell between us for a moment.

"That'd work, you know," he offered casually, his attention on the river. "With the coast being so close and everything. And maybe, if you wanted, you could even come by Santa Lucina from time to time."

A smile pulled at my lips and I felt myself starting to blush. "I'd like that."

He nodded, keeping his gaze on the water, though his lip

twitched as well. On the shore, Maddox had finished with the bag, and was now standing with Baylie, discussing pointers for campus while Daisy investigated the nearby bushes.

Seconds slid past. Absently, I played with the edge of the picnic blanket, trying to figure out how to ask the question without ruining the moment.

"So," I started, "have you told anyone? You know, about me?"

Noah didn't respond. I glanced at him.

Expression fading from his face, he watched his brother. "No, not yet."

I hesitated. "Could you maybe not?"

He looked over at me.

"I don't want people treating me like a freak," I explained awkwardly.

"They won't."

"But–"

"Really. My dad, my brother, we all grew up with my grandfather's stories. Even Diane has heard them. And we're not…" He trailed off, as though changing his mind about the words. "It'd be better if they knew. Better for you, better for me. I don't want to lie to them, and you…" He grimaced. "I heard the crap that guy was yelling at the house. 'Landwalker'. That's not something your average intruder says. So he's one of them, isn't he? Both him and that Jesse guy."

I hesitated, and then nodded.

"Do you have any idea why they're after you?"

I shook my head.

He sighed. "It'd help if my family knew about you. Knew what we were dealing with."

Discomfort moving through me, I dropped my gaze to the picnic blanket.

"You're not a freak, Chloe," he said quietly. "It's hard, finding out you're not quite what you always thought you were. But you're not a freak."

I looked back up at him. He almost sounded like he understood.

"Maybe think about it?" he asked.

I nodded.

Doing the same, he glanced to the river. Baylie was laughing at something Maddox had said.

"Does she know?" Noah asked.

"No," I admitted.

He looked back to me.

"I tried to tell her, but I just… I didn't know what to say," I explained. "I don't really know anything about this."

"'Hi, I've just discovered spikes growing out of my arms. How are you?'"

A laugh escaped me. "Yeah. Something like that."

"Are you going to?"

My stomach twisted and I grimaced. I'd meant to. Planned to. Knew I should. And yet…

"You're not a freak, Chloe."

"Says you."

He reached over, putting a hand to my arm. "You're not."

I watched him for a moment, and then managed a nod.

"So," he started, a touch of awkward curiosity in his tone. "Have you ever… you know…"

He made a small gesture toward my legs.

I shifted uncomfortably on the blanket. "No."

He looked a bit surprised, but he said nothing as he returned his attention to Maddox and Baylie.

I hesitated. "I'm kind of scared to."

Noah glanced back to me.

"It's just…" I grimaced, wanting to explain even if I didn't know how. "It's terrifying, the idea of that happening. Me, changing into some *thing*. My legs just being… being *gone*. I know it sounds great on paper, being able to swim through the ocean like that or something, but…" I shook my head. "I don't want it. Any of it."

"Maybe it wouldn't be so bad once you tried?" he offered.

My shoulders rolled at the thought. "I don't want it," I said again.

His brow furrowed, but he just nodded.

Maddox and Baylie left the riverbank and walked over to us.

"You both about ready to go?" Maddox asked.

Noah nodded. We stood, and I helped shake out the blanket before we packed it away. Maddox swung the empty cooler bag onto his shoulder and in only a few moments, we were back on the trail.

"Okay," Baylie said to Maddox, as though continuing a topic from earlier. "But Dad's always telling me horror stories about how terrible the crime is around there. Like, how there are all these gangs and everything. I mean, I think he just wants me to go to Kansas State, but what about that? Is it *actually* that bad, or…?"

Noah hung back, looking away as the others moved on.

I paused, watching him.

"Whatever you say to Baylie," he said in a low voice, "let me tell my family about you. My grandfather's stories… He talked about magic, about all sorts of things. But he said your kind are strong, Chloe. *Very* strong. You'd have to be to get through the water like you do. And most of them… He claimed you barely sleep. You hardly even need to eat. You can go for days without both, if you have to. So these guys after you, they're going to be like that, and I just…" Noah shook his head. "I don't want to leave my family in the dark."

A pained expression crossed my face.

"Chloe…"

"But," I tried, feeling a bit desperate, "even if you tell them, it's not like the cops would believe them. It won't change anything."

He grimaced. "Wouldn't you rather know, if it was you?"

I looked away, hating that he was right.

"Hey, you guys coming?" Maddox called.

Noah raised a hand in wordless request for another moment.

"They won't treat you like a freak," he said. "I promise."

I closed my eyes. I didn't want this. Any of it.

"Please, Chloe."

"Okay."

He let out a breath. "Thank you."

I nodded.

He started down the trail. I followed, fighting hard not to imagine what could happen when the Delaneys discovered I was part fish.

We got back to the cabin later that afternoon, and Noah didn't waste any time. Drawing Diane and Maddox aside, he headed into the house to talk to them – and I knew that when Peter returned from dealing with the window repair in Santa Lucina, Noah would do the same with his father. Eyeing us all curiously, Baylie took the cooler bag back to the kitchen without a word. I sank down onto one of the log benches in the front yard and plucked at the nearby grass blades, trying to believe that Noah knew his family as well as he thought.

And that I wouldn't end up being stared at like a circus attraction for the rest of my time in this place.

Their talk didn't take long.

I looked up as the front door swung open and Diane came outside. She walked over to the bench, and gave me a smile as she sat down.

Watching her from the corner of my eye, I waited.

"So," she began.

I twisted a grass blade between my fingers.

"You know, when you showed up here on a bus like that, I wondered if you didn't have a good reason."

I didn't respond. She sighed.

"It's okay, honey," she said, putting a hand on mine and stilling my fingers on the grass. "There's nothing wrong with being different."

I hesitated. "I had to come back," I told her quietly. "Just out of nowhere, it was like I didn't have a choice. And when Mom and Dad tried to stop me, I just…"

Diane nodded. "I can imagine."

My brow furrowed in confusion.

"From the stories I've heard, I mean," she explained.

I looked down.

"About your parents, though," she continued. "When they came to get you, they told us you couldn't swim."

"I can't."

Her eyebrow climbed.

"I mean, I haven't. I've never been in the water before. Not even a pool. But I thought maybe the others could teach me."

"That was really dangerous, Chloe."

I grimaced. "I know. I just… I wanted to get out there so badly. And they never let me learn. They're so scared of everything to do with water."

"Do they know what you are?"

"I don't know."

She let out a breath, nodding. "Maybe we can talk to them."

I looked over at her, surprised.

Diane smiled. "If there's one thing I've learned in life, it's that there are all kinds of mysteries and wonders in this world. Some of us get to be them. Some of us get to be a part of them. But either way," her hand patted my knee, "they're not something we should fear."

On the porch, the screen door swung open and Noah came outside. Diane rose to her feet.

"You just let me know if you need to head back toward the coast, okay?" she said to me.

Feeling a bit dumbstruck, I nodded. She gave Noah another smile and then walked back to the house.

He came over and sat down. I could see the grin hovering around the edges of his mouth. I gave him a half-hearted glare.

"You want to say 'I told you so'?" I asked.

"Well… I did."

I shook my head. "How is it they're so okay with this?"

"Like I said—"

"Your grandfather's stories, I know. But those must have been *some* stories for you all to just… I mean…"

He shrugged, dropping his gaze to the grass. "Some stories are real."

"But most people aren't so ready to believe them."

"Most people aren't us."

I watched him, but he didn't look away from the ground.

The screen door opened and Baylie walked out onto the porch. "Hey, Diane wants to know if you guys want to do another cookout for dinner?"

Noah glanced up. "Sounds good," he called.

"Okay, she…"

Baylie trailed off, her attention locked on something beyond us. I turned as the sound of tires on gravel carried up the hillside.

My parents' car was pulling into the driveway.

A sinking feeling hit me, bringing with it a sense of panic I was starting to know well.

I'd wanted them to take me back. I'd wanted to get out of here, and on some level, a tiny part of me still did. But now, with the Delaneys knowing what I was and being so miraculously okay with it…

The sedan came to a stop. My mom thrust open the driver's side door instantly.

I blinked. She looked terrible. Her brown hair was a tangle and her face seemed haggard, like she hadn't slept in a week. On the edge of the car door, her fingers clutched the metal as though it was all that kept her upright. In the passenger seat, my father didn't even move, and despite the shadows in the sedan, I could still see the dark circles under his eyes.

"Get in the car," Mom ordered.

I heard the cabin's screen door open and I glanced back to

see Diane come outside.

"Chloe," my mom snapped. "I won't ask again. Get–"

"Hey Linda," Diane called, her welcoming tone at odds with the tension in the yard. "I'm so glad you all could make it. You have any trouble finding the place?"

Mom blinked and turned an expression on the woman that was almost hunted. "Fine." She looked back to me. "Chloe, car."

Watching her warily, I rose to my feet, moving no closer. Beside me, Noah did the same.

"You don't have to run out so fast," Diane said.

Mom's gaze snapped to her. "It's fine. We just–"

"What's going on, mom?" I interrupted.

"We're leaving."

I hesitated. Up on the porch, I could see Baylie watching us all.

"No," I said.

Mom's face flushed angrily.

"Not until you explain," I finished.

Her gaze swept the others. "I'm not having–"

"Baylie," Diane interrupted. "Would you go check that we have enough hotdogs for dinner?"

Brow furrowing, Baylie eyed us for a moment, and then retreated into the cabin.

"It's okay, Linda," Diane said, coming down the porch stairs. She glanced back as the door closed. "We know."

Mom's eyes widened, and she looked between me and

Diane.

"Tell me what's going on, Mom. Please."

She stared at me, and then cast a look back into the car. In the passenger seat, my dad hung his head.

"Chloe," she tried. "We just need to—"

Dad said something to her, so low I couldn't hear, but at the words, she paused, a desperate expression flashing across her face. She shook her head at him.

He pushed open the door.

I swallowed hard. He looked even worse than her.

"Is there somewhere we can talk with our daughter?" he asked Diane, his voice hoarse.

She nodded. "Inside," she said, sounding taken back.

He stepped away from the car. My mom rushed around to the passenger side, coming to support him. With a tired gesture, he waved her off.

Staring at them both, I followed them to the cabin.

"You can use our room," Diane said to my dad as we came in.

He nodded and headed for the master bedroom, my mom reluctantly following.

Diane took my hand as I passed her. "We'll be outside if you need us," she assured me.

I nodded, giving her a small smile, and then trailed them through the doorway.

Mom had crossed the room to the window, and stood with one hand holding the curtain aside as she stared at the trees and the mountains. On the edge of the bed, Dad sank down with a sigh, and propped his elbows on his knees.

"Are you all okay?" I asked warily as I shut the door.

Mom turned back to me. "We're fine. We just need to–"

"Linda," Dad interrupted.

A pained look flickered over her face and she returned her gaze to the window.

"She said they knew," Dad continued to me. "What do they know, Chloe?"

I hesitated. "About me."

Mom closed her eyes. "You *told* me you didn't go in the water," she said, her voice choked.

"I-I didn't. I just…"

A grimace twisted my face. I didn't know where to begin about Jesse, the intruders at the Delaneys' house, or that night on the beach with Zeke – and I wasn't sure I wanted to. It wasn't the point. None of this was the point, because clearly they knew the truth.

And they'd never said anything.

They'd made up stories about dangers in the ocean. They'd punished me for looking at pictures of the sea, for wanting to go swimming, or for even touching the neighbor's garden hose. They'd done all they could to keep me from every drop of water in the world.

And they'd never once told me the truth about why.

Anger built up in my chest, making it hard to breathe.

"We told you it wasn't safe," Mom said.

I trembled.

"You should have obeyed us," she continued. "Then we wouldn't be in this position."

A breath escaped me.

"Chloe–"

"You lied!" I shouted.

She blinked. "We–"

"You *lied* to me! All those years, and you just – who *are* you? Are you guys dehaian? Are you something else? What the *hell* is going on that made you just lie and lie and never once tell me anything about–"

"Chloe!" Dad yelled.

I cut off, breathing hard.

"You're right," he said more quietly.

I stared at him. By the window, Mom turned away.

"You're right," he repeated. "We did lie. And we should have told you the truth a long time ago."

He looked down at his hands. "How did you find out? Your mother said something about a boy?"

My brow furrowed as I tried to regroup. "Yeah. Zeke. He saved me. When I fell overboard."

He nodded, not taking his gaze from his folded hands. "Did you change at all?"

I shifted my weight, suddenly uncomfortable at talking about that part of things with my father. "H-he said I started to. I don't remember."

Dad drew a breath. "And he told you about this then?"

"Later. After the… after the hospital. I went onto the beach and he was there. He showed me the, um, other stuff. Some of it. But I didn't go in the water," I added to Mom. "Just to the edge of it."

On the curtain, her hand tightened.

"But I don't understand," I continued. "You guys aren't… I mean, you're sick. You hate it here." I paused. "You're not like me at all."

Dad looked away.

"You…" he started. "Your mom and I…"

"We adopted you," Mom said, her voice choked.

I stared at her, hearing the words though they made no sense.

"When you were born," Dad filled in. "We adopted you then."

My mouth opened, but whatever had wanted to emerge just evaporated before becoming sound.

"Your birthmother was my sister," he continued. "She was… she got involved with someone she shouldn't have. And when it came time for you to be born… she died."

Everything felt numb. My arms and legs were thick and weird, and every motion or action I could think to take just seemed artificial, like I was an actor in some absurd play we were all suddenly carrying out.

"We knew we'd have to tell you someday," he said. "We just… we wanted to wait for the right time."

A gasping laugh escaped me.

"Chloe," Mom tried.

The laugh took on the edge of a shriek, and I cut it off, digging my nails into my palms.

"We always wanted children," Dad said. "But we never could have any of our own. And when Susan – your birth-mother – died, we couldn't leave you to some child welfare system. Not with what we knew you'd have to deal with."

I looked over at him, my brow furrowing.

"Your father was a dehaian named Kreyus," Dad explained. "And Susan, Linda, me... we're something else. Like you said, we don't do well near the ocean." He grimaced. "We're called landwalkers. And basically, we're the dehaians' opposites. We used to be the same, used to live in the ocean like they do, but there was... a situation. Our ancestors and theirs messed with powers they shouldn't have, and as a result, our people split into two groups. Dehaians who have to stay by the ocean, and landwalkers who can't come near it. Our abilities and every-thing that made us like them went away, and for us even the shortest time in proximity to the sea can be damaging now. We have medicines that can get us close to the ocean for brief periods, but they..." He glanced to Mom. "They come with serious side effects, and only serve to delay the pain.

"Susan liked to push the limits, though," he continued. "She always was something of a wild child. And on one of her adventures, she met a dehaian who claimed to be doing the same. They were only together for a little while, before the effect of the ocean drew Kreyus back and drove her away. But when she returned home, she was pregnant with you."

The ground felt unsteady, and all my breaths seemed to be coming in short gasps. Swallowing hard, I forced my voice to work, though the sound that emerged was nothing like what I was used to hearing. "And she... she died?"

"I'm so sorry."

"W-what about him? Did he ever...?"

Dad looked down briefly. "Susan never told us anything beyond his name."

I trembled, wanting to sit down, run away, or do something that made more sense than this conversation.

Than some other dad-thing being out there somewhere.

"But why... why'd you never...?"

He drew a breath. "We thought it would be better if you didn't know. We were just trying to keep you safe."

I stared at him, uncomprehending.

Dad grimaced. "Children of dehaians and landwalkers to-gether... sweetheart, they almost never survive. Most of them are stillborn or die as babies. The two sides of their ancestry just can't coexist inside one person. And even if the children *do* manage to live long enough to grow up at all, there's still the fact that sooner or later the two halves will become unbalanced." He sighed. "We used to be dehaian. That side is stronger. Eventually, it begins to emerge and draws them to the ocean... but the change is too much for them. It sends their systems into shock." His brow furrowed. "And they die."

Air pressed from my chest.

"We thought," Dad continued, "that if we kept you away from the water, maybe you'd stay safe. And for the longest time, it seemed like it was working. You were just so... so *fine*. Not hurt by the distance from the sea, not sick or anything. And we wanted that for you. Just... for you to be okay. We love you, Chloe. I know it hasn't always looked like it, but we do. But we worried that if we let you anywhere near water, even brought up anything about the ocean at all, it would wake that side in you. Start making you more like one of them. And maybe kill you."

I shuddered and my hand grasped the edge of the dresser by the bedroom door. I'd passed out at Noah's house after the boat capsized. I'd felt so weird, so shaky and so warm.

And I could have died. I really, *actually* could have died.

My stomach rolled and I swallowed hard. "You should have told me. I could have... I might have..."

"We just wanted to wait for the right time."

"*When?*" I cried, looking back at him. "When I was thirty? *Fifty?* I..." Tears stung my eyes and furiously, I swiped them away. "A dehaian tried to *kill* me, Dad! And if... if I'd *known...*"

I turned away, shaking. This was too much. Too stupid and too much. I couldn't handle this.

"We didn't know there were dehaians who would try that, Chloe," he said. "I promise. And if we had, we... we would have said something. We've only ever tried to protect you. Honest."

I didn't turn back around. They would have warned me about robbers, or rapists, or something else of that kind. But not fish-people with glowing eyes. I knew that much.

Even if I didn't know anything else anymore.

My hand tightened on the edge of the dresser.

I'd daydreamed about them not being my parents, but it'd just been a stupid fantasy. Every kid did that at some point. And yeah, I'd wanted to be near the ocean, but besides them and their 'landwalker' people or whatever, who didn't?

Though come to think of it, that guy who'd broken into the Delaneys' house had called me that. He'd said something about landwalker whores, and he'd–

"Chloe," Mom tried.

The sound of her voice was like a barb straight into my side, and I gasped.

"You need to understand," she said. "You're *our* daughter. You belong with *us*. We've only ever done what was best for you, and if we'd told you about Susan, and about that man she was with, that dehaian side of you might have–"

I couldn't take it. My hand went for the handle and I yanked open the door before she'd finished speaking.

"Chloe!" Dad called after me.

I raced across the living room, ignoring him. On the log bench, Noah and Diane looked up in shock as I burst past the front door. Grabbing at the rail, I took the steps at a run and bolted for the forest the moment I hit the ground.

At my back, I could hear people calling my name. But I

didn't want to talk to them. To anyone. I just wanted away from here. Away from this. Away from landwalkers and dehaians and everything that had been the past weeks, months, and years of my life.

Trees blurred as I dashed up the hiking trail. My shoes pounded over the uneven dirt as I climbed the hills and skidded down the slopes as fast as my feet could carry me. Tears burned in my eyes, further disfiguring the trees and the blue sky, and gasping, I raked them away and pushed myself to keep going.

Time passed. My sides started to cramp and my lungs burned. Choking on air, I slowed and finally let myself look around.

The river was just beyond the next curve of the trail.

Breathing hard, I stared at the path, and then glanced back. It'd taken us three hours to get here before. And yes, we'd been hiking slowly, and yes, I didn't know how long I'd been running, but still…

Strong, Noah had said. Dehaians were strong.

And if I let myself become like them, I'd die.

Holding back a sob, I wrapped my arms around my middle as I walked toward the river.

Sunlight glinted off the tumbling water, but near to where we'd had lunch, a cluster of trees shaded a pile of rocks. Trembling, I headed for them. The boulders were rough beneath my hands as I climbed to the uppermost rock, but they still felt blessedly stable and real. I sat down and drew my legs up, hugging my knees to my chest as I watched the water rush by.

I couldn't go home and I couldn't go near the ocean. My parents weren't my parents and I had no idea what to call them anymore. A few days ago, a madman had tried to kill me, and I didn't even know why.

Closing my eyes, I pressed my forehead to my knees.

The sound of footsteps came from the trail. Flinching, I looked up.

Noah jogged around the turn, only to stop at the sight of me. Tugging out his phone, he hit a number and then raised the cell to his ear.

"I found her," he said. "She's fine."

He waited a moment and then hung up. Returning his phone to his pocket, he walked closer, not taking his eyes from me.

"Chloe?"

I didn't respond. For all I knew, that wasn't even my real name.

The thought hurt. My arms tightened around my legs, trying to squeeze it away.

Cautiously, he sank onto one of the rocks, and from the corner of my eye, I could see him watching me. Thoughts chased themselves across his face for a moment, and then his brow furrowed and he turned to the water.

And said nothing.

My gaze slid to him as the seconds crept by. There wasn't

any expectation in the way he was sitting there. No impatience either. He just looked like one of the rocks, content to wait forever till I wanted to speak.

If I decided to at all.

My eyes closed as a choked feeling grew in my throat. Water rushed past the rocks, babbling nonsensically.

"They adopted me," I whispered.

I looked down to see his head turn toward me, though he didn't try to meet my eyes.

"M-my mother... she was Dad's – I mean, my..."

The words wouldn't come. I didn't know what they would even be.

"His sister," I finished. "She was his sister. And when I was born, she died."

A rough breath entered my lungs. "She was a landwalker. Someone who can't come near the ocean. And my... my dad was a dehaian. But kids from parents like that, they die. They always die. Even if they survive long enough to grow up a bit, the water pulls them back. And then when they try to change... the shock kills them."

Noah didn't seem to be breathing. Motionless on the boulder, he sat, his eyebrows twitching down spasmodically.

"I'm not going to be able to stay away, though. I-I know I'm not. I want to, but it just... it hurts to even think about leaving. But if I don't–"

"You don't have to," he said, his voice tight.

I looked down at him.

"You've survived this so far. The spikes, the boat capsizing – you even survived that bastard in the bookstore. You ran from the cabin faster than I've ever seen anyone move, and you've held out against the pull of the water ever since you came back to town."

He turned, looking up at me. "They don't know that. They just see other people and stories that make them afraid. But you're stronger than they realize, Chloe. And you've already survived becoming more dehaian than they know."

"But at your house... I just collapsed. I–"

"For a moment, sure. And maybe that was the shock they were talking about. But you woke up almost immediately and you haven't collapsed since. Not when the spikes came out, not when your eyes glowed. You're already changing, and maybe it's just the tip of the iceberg, but it's still something and you're still alive."

He reached up, taking my hand. "You can survive this. I know you can."

My gaze lingered on his fingers around mine. He sounded so certain, so confident where no one else had.

I trembled. I was afraid he wasn't right – I'd only ever changed a bit, and even that had been overwhelming – but I couldn't say that. After one week, he had more faith in me than my parents, or whatever they were, had possessed in their entire lives.

And right now, that felt more precious than gold.

My eyes tracked up, meeting his deep green gaze, and I gave

him a small nod. Echoing the motion, he looked back at the river.

Seconds slid past with the water.

"You want to head back?" he asked quietly.

"Not really."

He glanced up at me, his mouth twitching into a smile, and after a moment, I managed a tiny one as well.

His hand still wrapped around mine, we sat in silence and watched the river roll by.

16

ZEKE

The beach was still several miles away when I caught sight of the guards. A dozen of them sped through the water, and as I raced to catch up, my brow rose at the other person accompanying them.

"Niall!" I yelled.

He looked toward me as I swam closer.

"What're you doing here?" I asked. "Ren just said he was sending the guards."

Niall grinned as I pulled up alongside him. "What, and let my little brother have all the fun? Damsel in distress, psychotic cult… Seriously, you expect me to pass that up?"

I chuckled.

"So, you really saw Sylphaen?" he continued. "I mean, you're *sure?*"

"Oh yeah. Claimed they were the fourth sanctum of them or whatever. Which is just great, because it means there're more out there."

"Yeah, fantastic. But why are they after this girl?"

"Not sure. They think she's some kind of monster or something. Kept calling her a 'creature', saying she wasn't dehaian even though I saw her change – or start to, anyway. But they're trying to kill her. Drug her up and then sacrifice her, to be specific."

Niall's expression became flabbergasted. "That's sick."

"No kidding. There *is* something strange about her, though. When she touches the ocean... you can feel it, Niall. It's like electricity in the water."

His eyebrows climbed.

The foremost guard signaled that Santa Lucina was in view, and we slowed.

"Where to?" Niall asked me.

"The house is just north of that park Ina likes."

"House?"

I nodded.

Niall's brow shrugged. "Okay, you heard him," he called to the guards.

They took off. We followed.

"So," I started, "Ren was okay with you heading out here?"

He hesitated. "Well... you know how he is."

"So that's a no."

"I didn't tell him."

"Ah."

Niall grinned. "He'll get over it."

The water became shallower. One of the guards rose to the

surface quickly, and checked around before diving again. He motioned for the others to fan out to either side, and then led the way to the beach.

We broke through the waves and left the ocean. A curve of the bluffs obscured much of the park and I couldn't see anyone on the rocky stretch of beach below the house. The lead guard motioned for several of his people to keep watch on the sands while the rest of us headed for the steps.

"You think she'll be here?" Niall whispered.

I shrugged. "This is where she was staying."

"And the Sylphaen?"

I met his gaze briefly. "Said something about Plan B."

We climbed the stairs to the yard, and then paused as the guard reached the top. He scanned the lawn and the mansion windows, and then hurried for the wall of bushes that ringed the house. Niall followed, while the remaining guards circled to the opposite side of the yard.

I looked to the windows, but I couldn't see anything moving behind them. It was possible she wasn't home. That they'd gone into town or something.

Nothing said the Sylphaen had found her already.

Hanging onto the thought, I continued after Niall. Scales hardened the soles of my feet as we slipped into the brush surrounding the mansion. The bramble was wide enough to mostly shield us from view on either side of the hedge and, moving as silently as possible, we followed it onward. From the front of the house, I could hear voices rising over the sound of hammering, their words indistinguishable. As the driveway came into view, I spotted a truck with advertisements for window repair on its side. A few workers stood near it, while another was talking with the man I'd seen in the waiting room when Chloe was hurt.

The man from the hospital gestured toward the window. The repairman turned.

I froze. It was one of the behemoths that Kirzan had ordered to watch me.

This couldn't be good.

"Him," I whispered to Niall. "He's one of them."

Niall nodded and then looked to the guards. They spread out, still watching the Sylphaen.

For a moment, the Sylphaen studied the repair work, looking for all the world like a contractor evaluating a project. Nodding a bit, he said something to the man from the hospital, who nodded in return. The Sylphaen shook the other man's hand and then turned, walking toward the side of the house and carefully scrutinizing the windows as he went.

Until he passed beyond the view of the driveway. Like an actor leaving a stage, he dropped any pretense of caring about the mansion and strode straight for the steps at the rear of the yard.

We ducked back through the bushes and hurried after him.

The Sylphaen jogged down the staircase, getting all the way to the beach before we reached the steps.

And then he heard us.

He looked back, catching sight of us at the top of the stairs, and alarm shot across his face. Without hesitation, he raced toward the ocean.

Guards rose from the water, cutting him off. The others ran down the stairs ahead of me and grabbed the man as he attempted to bolt. With ruthless efficiency, they yanked his arms behind his back and took his legs from under him, sending him face-first down to the sand. Another guard hauled him partially up again, wrapping an arm around the man's throat. The Sylphaen struggled in their grip, snarling curses, and then he spotted Niall and me behind the guards.

Fury suffused his expression. "You treacherous little—"

"Save it," I told him. "Where's Chloe? Have your people found her yet?"

He sneered.

"Answer the question, scum," Niall ordered, and I glanced back to see him jerk his chin at the guards.

Spikes emerged from the forearm of the guard holding the Sylphaen's neck, the barbs pressing into the man's skin and coming perilously close to breaking it.

Hatred joined the anger on the Sylphaen's face. "Foul spawn of—"

"Do you have Chloe?" I snapped.

The Sylphaen was silent for a moment, and then his sneer returned. "All is according to our plan, and no creature will stop us now."

"What the hell does that mean?" I demanded.

The hatred in the man's eyes grew stronger as he glared up at me. "We have prepared for this day for generations. Our resources are vast beyond what your petty mind can imagine. And they have delivered us the creature's location. Simple cell phone tracing is not out of our reach, and these foolish animals have given no question to the equipment we brought along." His lips curled back in disgust. "All who stand against us are fools, but we will rid the world of you. The abomination will be ours within the hour. Nothing you can do will stop that."

"*Damn*, you babble," Niall commented.

"Where is she?" I said, still watching the Sylphaen. "Where are your people headed?"

His sneer deepened.

I glanced to the guard. The man pushed the spikes into the Sylphaen's skin, bringing droplets of blood to the surface.

The Sylphaen's face tightened and his gaze went from me to Niall and back. "Nothing can stop us," he said contemptuously. "Long live the Wisdom."

He thrust his throat onto the guard's spikes.

"What the hell?" Niall cried.

The guard stumbled back, staring at the Sylphaen. Blood poured from the wounds on the man's neck, even as contempt still tried to twist his face. His eyes widened as he choked, and then went still.

I stared.

"That… what…" Niall tried. He drew a sharp breath and looked to the guards. "Get… get that out of here."

The guards bent to gather the body.

I turned away, blinking in shock. The guy had just…

"Zeke," Niall said, still sounding shaken.

Air entered my lungs. I looked back at him.

"We're not going to be able to find her without…" He shook his head. "We should head back to the water. Have the guards watch–"

"No. No, we can't just…"

My gaze went to the top of the bluffs. That guy. The one from the hospital. If we could talk to him, maybe we could warn her before they got too close.

I ran back up the stairs.

"Zeke?" Niall called.

He chased after me.

Reaching the yard, I kept moving, not bothering to hide anymore. Racing around the corner of the house, I took in the missing truck and the absent workers, and then caught sight of the man pulling out from the far end of the driveway in his car.

"Hey!" I called, running after him.

He was already taking off down the street.

I stopped at the end of the drive, watching him disappear around the next turn. Snarling a curse, I looked back as Niall came jogging up behind me.

"He could have warned her," I said.

Niall's expression mirrored my own. "They still have to bring her back to the ocean," he pointed out.

I grimaced, my skin crawling at the idea of them getting their hands on her at all.

"We should fan out," Niall continued. "Leave one guy here, and then head north with half the rest and send the others south. Try to cover as much of the coast as possible, so no matter where they—"

"This is where they've been, though. They're all here."

"Doesn't mean they'll come back this way, especially since this is where people know her and will be looking for her if they learn she's been kidnapped." He paused. "The Sylphaen can get her in the water anywhere. Trying here is probably their worst choice."

I looked away. He might be right. But I couldn't shake the feeling that they would come back to Santa Lucina again. The dead one on the beach had been here, along with potentially more, and they must have stuck around for a reason.

"Send the guards in either direction along the coast," I said. "But I'm staying."

"Zeke—"

"That guy on the beach was here for a reason."

"Maybe to make sure none of her friends rushed off to help."

"Or to be a lookout." I exhaled, trying to calm down. "Come on, Niall. I'm not saying you're wrong, I just want to keep an eye out around here."

His mouth tightened. "Okay, then I'm staying too."

I nodded. "Thanks."

He echoed the motion. We walked back to the stairs.

On the beach, the guards were waiting, though the Sylphaen's body was gone. I looked out at the water, knowing one of them must have dragged him out there to be lost in the currents.

"You three," Niall called, jerking his chin at several of the guards as he reached the bottom of the steps. "You stay with us. The rest, I want you to split up. Half to the north, half south, and cover as much space as possible. You feel this electricity-in-the-water thing Zeke talked about, you signal."

They gave a nod and headed for the waves.

Niall glanced back at me. "We should stay oceanwise. Better view of more shoreline that way."

I made a noise of agreement, and then followed him into the tide.

If the Sylphaen brought her into the water anywhere near us, I'd feel it. And if they tried it anywhere else, one of the guards along the coast would be able to tell. It was hard to miss, that strange thing she did when she touched the water.

I just hoped we caught them, because I didn't want to imagine what those bastards had planned.

17

CHLOE

"But then my dad comes home, and Maddox just takes off! Leaves me standing there, in a bathroom covered in mud and holding this sopping wet puppy, like it was all my idea to take the poor thing in!"

I laughed and Noah grinned. Pushing a branch out of our way, he waited for me to pass him.

"So what'd you do then?" I asked as we continued down the trail toward the cabin.

"Well... panic. I dropped the puppy into the bathwater and tried to grab a towel, but the little guy just jumped out of the tub and bolted through the door. Next thing I know, I hear my dad yelling because this wet dog is racing around the living room."

"Ouch."

"Yeah, I ended up grounded for about a week over that one."

"And Maddox?"

Humor showed in Noah's eyes. "Two weeks, mostly for running off on me."

I laughed again. "How old were you guys?"

He thought for a moment. "Eight, maybe? So Maddox would've been eleven. Yeah, that sounds about right."

"What happened to the dog?"

"Oh, turns out he wasn't a stray after all. Some neighbors down the street had been looking for him all afternoon." He grinned. "And they were really grateful we'd given him a bath so they didn't have to."

I shook my head, still smiling. We walked around the turn of the trail, and the rear of the cabin came into view.

Gunshots rang out from the far side of the house.

I froze, my mind trying to catch up with my ears. Screams rose on the heels of more gunfire, along with the sound of shattering glass and Daisy barking.

Noah ran for the cabin.

I gasped and took off after him.

A man in a black ski mask darted around the side of the house. At the sight of Noah racing toward him, he skidded, his eyes going wide.

His arm raised.

I screamed.

And the gun fired.

Noah stopped as the bullet hit him. His hand clutched at his chest and his body jerked, as though he was choking around the pain. Doubling over, he staggered a step, and then crashed to the ground.

I stared. This couldn't be happening. This wasn't–

The man charged at me faster than anyone had the right to move.

Tearing my gaze from Noah, I stumbled away and ran.

The man's fingers snagged my hair and yanked me backward, sending pain shrieking through my scalp. I screamed and clawed at his grip as he dragged me to the ground.

"Get the hell away from her!"

At the cry, the man suddenly stumbled and his fist vanished from my hair. Twisting on the ground, I scrambled back and looked up.

My mom had jumped on him. Like a wild woman, she had her arm wrapped around his throat as she desperately tried to choke him. Her other hand tore at his ski mask, blinding him momentarily and making him cry out with rage.

Grabbing at her, he caught her shirt and arm, and then ripped her from him and hurled her to the ground.

She hit the dirt path hard and rolled. Her hands landed on a rock and with a cry, she flung it at his head.

He dodged the stone.

And pulled out his gun.

"No!" I shouted.

The man paused. His head turned and his eyes met mine while Mom scrambled to the side.

His gun tracked her.

"Don't," I pled.

Beneath the torn ski mask, his mouth twitched toward a snarl.

"What do you want?" I continued desperately. "Me? I'll go with you. Just please don't."

His expression became disgusted. Beyond him, I could see Mom, still in the line of his handgun.

I trembled. He'd shoot her. I knew he would. He'd shot Noah and no one else had come around the side of the house this entire time. It was just us and him and...

My forearms stung as the spikes grew.

"Chloe, no..." Mom begged.

"I'm not a landwalker," I tried, ignoring her. "See? I don't know why you're doing this, but I'm not-"

"We know exactly what you are."

I hesitated. "O-okay. But please, you don't have to do this."

"Yes we do."

There was nothing in his voice. Just cold certainty and it left me shaking. He looked back at Mom, taking aim again.

Something slammed into him, knocking his shot wide and propelling him from the path. The man screamed, flying through the air and then crashing into a tree trunk. He tumbled to the ground and didn't move again.

I stared.

It was Noah. But not. Alive and well, he stood with his back to me, regarding the crumpled man he'd just thrown into the tree. Smoke rose from his fists and cracks like fissures in stone ran up his arms, with fiery light like molten lava coming from

AWAKEN

inside them.

He turned, looking at me. His eyes glowed red like coals, and more cracks surrounded them, radiating outward like jagged tattoos of light. Blood stained his shirt, the wetness centered on a hole torn near the middle of his chest, and beneath the fabric, his skin shone.

Motionless, he watched me, and nothing human was in his gaze.

And then he drew a breath, tensing briefly as the fissures began to fade.

"Are you alright?" he asked as his eyes darkened back to their normal green.

A gasp of air entered my lungs. On the path behind him, Mom pushed to her feet, not taking her eyes from him. He glanced over at her, and then back at me.

I couldn't stop staring.

"We have to go," he said.

My head nodded on its own. Reaching out, he extended a hand to me. My gaze dropped to his palm, and after a moment's hesitation, I took it.

He felt the same. Warm, with skin no different than a short time ago.

His fingers wrapped around mine and he drew me up from the ground.

"What are you?" I whispered as the spikes retreated from my arms.

Noah paused. "It's complicated. Come on."

Bringing me with him, he headed for the cabin.

"Keep pressure on it!"

Diane's cry carried past the house as we came closer. Noah leaned his head around the corner, and then pulled me after him as he ran into the front yard.

The porch steps were a wreck, and two ski-masked men had been shoved into the debris. Several yards away, Dad lay on the grass with Diane crouched over him, pressing a bundle of towels to his shoulder. With Daisy at her feet, Baylie huddled nearby, clasping her upper arm while blood dripped past her fingers.

Mom pushed by me. "Bill? Bill, are you–"

"He's alive," Diane said as Mom kneeled by her side. "Ambulance is on its way."

Trading places with Mom, she rose to her feet and turned to me and Noah, hesitating as she saw the stains on his shirt.

"What happened?" Noah asked.

"Someone started shooting at us from the woods," Diane told him. "And then a bunch of men in masks came out of the brush at us. Maddox stopped those two, but the rest took off."

"Where is–" Noah started.

Maddox ran from the forest. Torn fabric and blood marred his shirt, and hair-thin cracks of firelight still shone in his skin, fading as I watched. His gaze raked the yard, catching on Noah.

"Any more of them?" he demanded.

Noah shook his head. "Only one came back there."

Maddox glanced his brother over and swiftly seemed to conclude what had happened. "I got three of them," he said, his voice nearly a growl. "The other two…"

Noah looked to the woods as the sound of sirens carried up the hillside.

"Get inside and change clothes before the ambulance arrives," Diane ordered. "Both of you."

The guys hesitated. Twitching his head at his brother, Maddox motioned for Noah to go in while he paused at the ruined stairs.

"How're we going to explain–" Maddox began, gesturing to the wreckage and the men inside.

"We don't," Diane said. "We say something hit them. We don't know what. Blame it on the others shooting at us."

He nodded. Noah pulled himself up onto the porch and then disappeared into the house.

My eyes went to Dad lying on the ground. Mom had a towel still pressed to his shoulder, but he was speaking to her, his voice too quiet to hear. Diane stood nearby, watching them and the road that the ambulance would drive equally.

I bit my lip, and then walked over to where Baylie sat on one of the log benches, her free hand absently stroking Daisy's fur. She flinched as I came near, as though I'd startled her, and when I lowered myself onto the bench next to her, she swallowed hard, looking bloodlessly pale.

"You okay?" I asked quietly.

She shivered. "W-we were just talking. And then suddenly there was all this noise. Your dad fell. Something hit my arm. It hurt so much and then these guys just…" Shaking her head, she didn't take her gaze from the ground. "I thought they were going to kill us. I thought…"

A frightened expression came over her face. "M-Maddox, though. He…" Her terrified eyes met mine for the first time. "Chloe, he changed. I swear. H-he just became some… *thing*. Like a monster. He threw two of them through the stairs and when the others tried to shoot him… he just went after them. He barely even stumbled. And his skin…"

Her trembling grew stronger and her gaze dropped to the grass, though she didn't seem like she was seeing it.

I swallowed and turned away. On the porch, Noah came outside and, at a quick nod from him, Maddox headed into the house.

Like they were trading off watch.

A shiver ran through me. They thought those guys might come back. They thought they might have to defend against them again.

Become those… things… again.

And they both were staying ready for it.

I glanced to Diane. She knew. Had known all along. And so of course my problems hadn't seemed strange.

She had two stepsons who could probably glow in the dark.

I looked back at Noah, my brow furrowing with hurt. He could have told me. He *should* have. I mean, everyone was entitled to secrets, but there I'd been, sharing this terrifying new discovery of spikes and scales and possible death, and he'd never said a word about the fact he wasn't human either.

Not one word.

He'd just seemed like he'd understood how I felt the entire time.

My gaze returned to the driveway as an ambulance pulled up. He still should have said something. But instead, he'd lied to me. Maybe not outright – much – but by omission. He'd had a hundred chances to say something, and he'd not taken one of them.

He'd also saved my life.

I grimaced and turned to help Baylie to her feet. As the EMTs rushed over to my dad, I continued on with her, leaving Daisy by the bench and walking toward the second ambulance that was coming to a stop on the grass.

The middle-aged driver hopped out and jogged over to us, while his younger companion circled to the rear of the vehicle.

"Hey there, I'm Marty," the first man said, putting a hand to Baylie's elbow gently. "Let's take a look at that arm, shall we?"

He directed her toward the back of the ambulance, where I could hear the younger guy opening the doors.

I looked over my shoulder, watching two EMTs load my dad onto a stretcher. Mom hovered nearby, holding his hand as they got ready to carry him back to the ambulance. Another EMT was checking over the men inside the ruin of the porch steps, with Diane eyeing him from several feet away. Maddox lingered near the corner of the house, effectively keeping anyone from wandering back toward the trail, while Noah stood on the porch, studying the surrounding forest.

"You doing alright?"

I flinched. The older med tech who'd been helping Baylie stood nearby, and he smiled ruefully at my alarm.

"Sorry," Marty apologized. "Didn't mean to scare you. You've got some scratches there. Can I get you something for them?"

He gestured and I glanced down, seeing the bloodied scrapes on my palms and arms for the first time.

I swallowed. The man currently lying broken by a tree had dragged me to the ground after he'd shot Noah. I just hadn't noticed the damage then.

"Sure," I managed.

I followed him back to the rear of the ambulance, where Baylie was sitting on the step. The younger EMT stood near her, tying off a bandage around her arm.

"You were lucky," he told her.

She swallowed and then nodded. He gave her a warm smile before following Marty into the back of the ambulance to gather more bandages.

I sat down next to her.

"What do you think Maddox… you know… *is*?" Baylie whispered to me, half-glancing to the EMTs behind us.

I shook my head.

"He can't be human, though, right? I mean, humans don't do that. Glow and have all this stuff in their skin and put people through–" She caught herself and lowered her voice again. "–through porches like they're ragdolls. They can't."

She turned to me, renewed alarm coming over her face. "Do you think Noah is like that?"

I looked down, uncertain what to say.

"I-I mean, what if he and Peter and all of them are just–"

Something white flashed at the corner of my eye and she gave a muffled cry. A hand clamped to my mouth and yanked me backwards into the ambulance. I tried to scream, though the sound never made it out as my back hit the cold metal floor. The door of the ambulance slammed, and the grip on my mouth disappeared.

The younger EMT stood over me, a hand gripping a rail attached to the wall and the other pointing a knife to one side.

"Scream and she's dead," he said.

I slid my gaze over. Baylie lay next to me, her body limp and a white cloth on the floor beside her.

The ambulance engine started up. "Good to go, Colin?" Marty called from the front seat.

"Yep," he replied.

The ambulance rocked as Marty pressed down the accelerator and pulled the vehicle through a tight turn. Holding the rail, Colin didn't take his eyes from me.

"Bet you thought you were pretty smart, surrounding yourself with them," he said.

"Who?" I asked warily.

He smirked. "We'll get what we want from you. We've had centuries to prepare for this. To watch for this. It doesn't matter how you try to avoid it; you'll serve our purpose, just as ordained."

I stared at him.

"Quit the chatter and dose her already!" Marty called.

Colin's brow furrowed. "Wait, *now*? But what if she–"

"You want her causing us trouble under the water? Come on! We need her prepped for the ceremony and she needs something else to think about besides getting away."

Colin grunted disgustedly. Keeping the knife pointed at Baylie, he reached over and tugged open a small drawer set into the wall. His eyes didn't leave me as he stuck his hand into the drawer and then pulled out a syringe.

Heart pounding, I looked between the knife and the needle.

"Don't move…" he warned.

He bent down toward me.

I kicked out hard, my foot slamming into his crotch.

He shouted, staggering backward in the tight confines of the ambulance. His wrist hit the wall and the knife fell from his grip to clatter on the ground.

I scrambled up, but he was already coming at me again. My hands grabbed the first thing I could reach and hurled it at him.

The box of medical gloves bounced uselessly away.

He snarled and charged at me. I kicked at him again, and he snagged my leg. Shoving it sideways, he sent me off balance. I stumbled and then swung a fist at his face, but he just grunted and drove me back against the partial rear wall of the ambulance.

"What the hell's going on back there?" Marty shouted.

Colin's fingers wrapped around my throat. His other hand rose, holding the needle.

Stinging rushed through my forearms. Desperately, I rammed the spikes forward.

His eyes went wide and the syringe dropped from his grasp. Wet heat ran over my arm and soaked my shirt as he choked. Blood frothed past his lips and his expression became unbelieving.

The ambulance tilted as Marty slammed on the brakes. Colin tumbled away from me, a row of deep red holes ripped in his chest.

I stared, my spikes retreating again.

"You *bitch*!" Marty shouted.

Something heavy hit me from behind. I fell hard, landing on Colin. Scrambling across his body, I tried to put distance between myself and Marty.

He grabbed my hair, yanking my head backward.

The needle jabbed my neck.

I gasped, a dizzying rush of pressure hitting me, starting from my neck and surging outward. Sizzling energy surged through my skin, making me shriek, and I collapsed as he flung me to the ground.

Behind me, Marty scoffed. "Half-breed scum," he muttered. "I hope the Wisdom takes his time on you."

His footsteps clunked on the metal floor as he headed back to the front. The engine revved again.

I choked. My skin burned. I could feel my legs changing. The fabric of my shorts and shirt scraped on me like acidified sandpaper and the air was too thick. Too heavy. I couldn't breathe.

The ambulance rocked. Marty was driving again.

My hands grasped at the cold metal ground, trying to pull me toward the door. Gold dust shimmered on my arms and hands. Heaving, my lungs fought to breathe the air. My fingers curled, digging against the metal as spots swarmed over my vision, devouring the light.

This wouldn't happen.

I wouldn't die like this.

Tears stung my eyes as I clung to the thought, repeating it inside my head louder and louder till the words became a shout.

I wouldn't. I wouldn't do this now. This wouldn't happen. Would. Not. Happen.

The air grew thinner.

I gasped. The burning pain of fabric on my skin faded to a dull ache and the light from the ambulance windows returned in a rush. Trembling hard, I pushed up from the floor with hands that bore only traces of iridescence.

My gaze went to the front of the vehicle. The world was sharp – sharper than it had ever been. I could see everything, down to the tiny print on the medical machines strapped to the wall and Marty's pulse throbbing in his neck.

Spikes stung as they pushed from my arms again.

On shaking legs, I stepped around Colin, trying to ignore the way my stomach twisted at the sight of him. Against the wall, Baylie still lay, her chest rising and falling in steady rhythm.

My fingers balled into a fist. The spikes spread out straighter from my skin.

I crept toward the driver's seat and raised my arm, bracing myself to threaten him into stopping.

Marty caught sight of me in the rearview mirror.

His eyes went wide. "What the—"

He yanked the wheel sideways, sending me stumbling. The engine roared as he floored the pedal. Grabbing at the railing on the wall, I barely stopped myself from falling.

Gravity dragged at me as the ambulance raced down the road. Clutching at the rail, I fought to pull myself forward, closer to him.

Marty looked over his shoulder, checking on me, and then he swerved hard, throwing me back against the wall. The impact drove the air from my lungs. Electricity raced over my skin, trying to change it again.

"Keep fighting, you little half-breed bitch!" Marty yelled.

"You still won't stop this!"

He whipped the wheel around again, hurling me in the other direction and nearly breaking my hold on the railing.

"Do you have any idea what we're going to do to you? Any idea how the Wisdom is going to bleed you *dry?*"

I clutched at the rail and looked to the front.

Marty's eyes were locked on me in the rearview mirror.

But the ambulance was heading straight for a curve. And a tree.

I gasped.

"The Beast is coming for you," Marty snarled. "It's waited so long in the deep, and now—"

Metal screamed and glass shattered as the front of the ambulance crumpled and the world tilted. I tumbled forward, slamming into the wall, and boxes and bottles came after me, pelting me as the floor and I both crashed back down.

I opened my eyes.

The ambulance was still. Broken glass tinkled down from the front window behind me, and a hissing noise came from the engine. In a jumble on the floor near my legs, Baylie stirred groggily, her brow furrowing as she struggled to wake.

I leaned away from the wall and then froze, pain lancing through me as all my muscles protested in chorus. As if to compensate, tingles of electricity surged across my body, setting off the burn of transformation all over again. I choked as air clogged my lungs like soup – thick and impossible to breathe – and my fingers dug into the floor, fighting the change.

"You…"

I flinched and looked to the front.

Marty lay in the driver's seat, the tatters of an airbag in front of him and a splintered branch from the tree rammed through his chest.

Nausea raced up my throat at the sight.

Slowly, his head turned to the side and his eyes pinned me. "We…" he whispered. "We're everywhere. You'll never… escape us all."

His lips curled into a smile, and then a breath left him.

He went still.

I stared. Trembling shook me and I gasped, trying to breathe around the impossibly dense air.

"Chloe?" Baylie murmured, her eyes squeezed shut against the light. "What…"

I looked down at her. My skin was burning and everything hurt. Pressed against the floor, my hands trembled while my legs shimmered iridescently.

"Chloe! Baylie!"

My head snapped up at the sound of Noah's voice. The back door tore open, nearly leaving its hinges, and light flooded the inside of the ambulance.

"Holy…" he started. "Maddox, get in here!"

Noah clambered up the step and hurried toward us as Maddox rounded the corner of the ambulance.

"Here," Noah said, shoving Colin's body toward him.

Maddox grabbed the man's legs and yanked him backwards. With a disgusted look to the body as it tumbled to the ground, he climbed in after his brother.

"Can you get her out?" Noah asked him, nodding to Baylie.

Without a word, Maddox scooped her up and then turned in the tight confines to carry Baylie toward the door.

I shuddered, the air growing thicker. I dug my fingers into the icy metal as black spots swam across my sight.

Noah crouched in front of me. "Chloe? What happened? What'd they do to you?"

"In... injected... something. Can't..."

He caught me as I slumped to the side. Muscling me back upright, he pressed his hands to my face. "Focus, Chloe. Come on. Fight it."

I closed my eyes, struggling to do as he said. To breathe. To fight. To stay human.

And not die.

"Baylie's waking up," Maddox called from beyond the door.

"They've done something to Chloe," Noah shouted back. "Injected her with something."

I heard Maddox swear.

"Come on..." Noah urged me.

I choked and then gasped as the air thinned. The burning faded from my skin again, though quivers still shook me.

"That's right," he said, relief clear in his voice. "Breathe."

I opened my eyes. His gaze met mine.

He smiled. "Hey."

"Hey," I whispered.

"Can you move?"

I winced, pushing away from the wall with muscles that felt like they'd give out at any moment.

"What'd they give you?" he asked.

"I don't… Just keeps trying to make me–"

I gripped his arm as shivers ran through me.

"We need to get you to the water," Noah said.

I shook my head hard. "No, no I–"

"Chloe, we have to."

I looked over at him, and I could see the worry in his eyes. My legs quivered, threatening to collapse on me again.

Swallowing hard, I nodded.

With his arm supporting me, Noah helped me toward the ambulance door.

"Maddox," Noah called as we reached the step. "We need to get her out of here."

By the vehicle's side, Maddox looked up. Baylie sat on the ground next to him, blinking blearily with a hand to her head. "Take the car. Dad's on his way and I've called Diane. She's coming to get us."

Noah nodded and then turned, holding me as I climbed down. The ground swayed as I reached it, and my grip on his arm tightened.

Step by wobbly step, we made it across the country road to the car.

Shifting around, he lowered me into the seat and then shut

the door and ran for the driver's side. My head leaned over, resting on the window as I focused on keeping myself breathing.

The door slammed. The engine started. In a cloud of dust, Noah sent the car roaring away from the ambulance.

"Just hang in there," he urged. "Just hang on."

Shivering, I looked over at him. His hands clutched the wheel and beyond the windows, the trees swept past at high speed.

"Mom and Dad," I whispered. "The other ambulance. Were they…"

"They're fine. The other EMTs were as confused as us when those bastards took off."

I let out a breath in relief.

"And then you…" I pressed a shaking hand to my leg as it tried to change again. "You both came after us."

He glanced to me. "Yeah."

I paused. "What are you?"

He hesitated, returning his gaze to the road. "Save your energy, Chloe."

"Noah…"

He didn't answer.

"Please."

He grimaced. "Greliaran."

My brow furrowed.

"It's from some dead language," he continued reluctantly. "Means guardian or protector or something. We're kind of like you: we look human but aren't. Not quite, anyway. And we... I mean, we just..."

"Stop bullets," I said hoarsely as he trailed off.

He glanced to me again. "Yeah. Sort of." He paused. "I guess that's a plus."

His hands adjusted on the wheel. "I only found out I was like this a few months ago. Dad, Maddox, they started showing signs of it when they were both really young. But I... I just didn't. I thought maybe I hadn't inherited it. That maybe I could just be human like our mom and not have to deal with the stuff they did. Hide things the way they did. But then, all of a sudden one day, there it all was. And I would have told you, but...we can't. Dad drilled that into us since we were kids. It's all secret, you see. It has to be, if we don't want to end up in a lab or something. Not even Baylie knows."

"But Diane..." I managed.

He sighed. "When Maddox was thirteen, he was hurt in a hit-and-run. Diane and Dad were around the back of the house; they heard it happen. They came running, found Maddox, and when his skin changed like ours does and he started healing up in front of her... Dad sort of had to explain." Noah gave a half-hearted chuckle. "She didn't really freak. Not too much, anyway. She was just pissed he hadn't shared it with her sooner. But then, Diane's awesome. He probably should have."

I watched him steer the car around another curve. The mountains were falling behind us and I could feel our proximity to the coast like a feather running over my skin, sending shivers through me.

"You don't have to be near the water, though," I whispered.

"It feels better," he admitted. "But it's not like it is for you."

I swallowed, leaning my head on the window again. The sense of the ocean nearby was getting worse. Making it harder to fight.

"Hang on," he urged. "We're almost there."

"Where are we going?"

"Home. Our stretch of beach is about as secluded as anything gets in town, so that's probably the safest place for you to…"

My eyes closed. I didn't want to think about it.

"You won't die, Chloe."

I looked over at him.

"You've made it this far," he insisted. "You won't."

I shivered. Up ahead, the outskirts of Santa Lucina came into view.

"And then what happens?" I whispered.

His brow furrowed.

"I-I change like they do. Then what?"

"You're better. Whatever they gave you gets out of your system, you change back, and you're fine."

I glanced to him. He didn't meet my eyes as he kept driving.

Biting my lip, I turned back to the window. The seat fabric hurt, and I shifted around on it, trying to make the burning stop. Filaments formed on my skin, tying my legs together and then snapping into smoke as I pulled them apart.

The car flew by fences and houses, rushing into town. Slowing to as far above the speed limit as he dared, Noah wove the sedan through the streets, cursing under his breath every time a stoplight appeared.

And finally, his house came into sight.

Pulling up fast in the driveway, he left the engine running and threw his door open the moment he could slam the gearshift into park.

I leaned my head back, fighting to keep the air from thickening.

The door flew open and his arms wrapped around me, lifting me up from the seat.

"I can walk," I protested hoarsely.

He ignored me. Shifting me around in his arms, he took off running.

Wind whistled in my ears as Noah circled the garage and raced through the backyard. His footsteps thudded on the wooden steps and then went silent when he reached the sand.

I could feel the saltwater in the air and I pressed my forehead to his shoulder, struggling desperately to keep my body from changing at the sensation.

He skidded to a stop with a curse.

I turned my head, following his gaze.

Dehaians were walking from the water. Scales melted from their legs as they moved, becoming swim trunks that shimmered faintly in the sunlight.

Noah's grip on me tightened.

"Chloe?" Zeke called, pushing past one of the men and running toward us through the waves.

"Who the hell?" Noah growled.

"He's not one of them," I whispered.

The words didn't make Noah relax.

Jogging onto the beach, Zeke started toward us and then slowed, his gaze going from Noah to me and back.

"We're here to help," he said cautiously. "We just need to get her in the water first."

Noah didn't move. "You all get the hell away from here, then. I'm not leaving her vulnerable with any of you around."

Zeke stared at him. "*Vulnerable?* Do you even know what she…" He grimaced. "Look, whoever you are, we don't have time for this. Did the Sylphaen dose her?"

"Leave."

"Dammit, did they dose her or is she just reacting to being out of the water this long?"

Noah paused. I swallowed in the thickening air, trying to force the words out.

He beat me to it. "They did."

Zeke muttered something in a language I'd never heard. "Get her in the water. Carefully, though. With what they gave her, too fast could be… bad."

Noah hesitated. A shudder rippled through me as my legs tried to change again.

Growling a curse, Noah headed into the water.

Saltwater spray hit me as the waves tumbled in around us, and I gasped, my body spasming in his arms. He clutched me tighter as tingles crawled over my skin and a cry escaped me at the feeling. My skin was changing. My hands flailed out, clutching at nothing, and I couldn't breathe in the stupid, dense, useless air.

"Easy," Noah urged, his voice tense.

He lowered me down.

I shrieked as the waves swept around me, over me, through me, tearing me apart. The water scorched my skin like acid and I thrashed in Noah's arms, trying to escape the pain while the ocean flooded down my throat, drowning me.

Noah clutched me tighter, holding me to his chest as my tears mingled with the saltwater.

And slowly, the world stopped hurting.

I gasped, my vision clearing. A sensation like a million tiny fingers caressing my skin ran over me, soothing the pain away. Blinking hard, I looked down at my body, afraid of what I would find.

My clothes were crumbling, as though a fire was burning them to dust despite the waves. Filaments of light shone through the vanishing fabric, twisting across my legs and chasing down toward my ankles and up across my chest, becoming iridescent, cream-toned scales as they passed. When the light reached my feet, it spread, transforming my flesh into a broad, translucent fin and bringing with it a feeling like unbearable pressure finally being released.

A breath escaped me. Lifting a hand, I watched the sunlight play across my shimmering skin. Nothing seemed as strange as I'd believed it would be.

Everything just felt right.

Noah shifted his grip slightly. I looked up.

From just above the rolling waves, he watched me.

I tensed, uncertain what he'd think now.

He seemed to feel my fear, and carefully, his arms adjusted around me. He pulled me back up through the water, his mouth curving into a smile.

My head broke the surface.

The air was too thick. It burned.

I gasped and jerked away. His hold broke and I fell into the water.

Horror swept over me. Fighting to stay balanced against the current, I turned, looking back up at him.

His expression mirrored my own.

Frantic, my gaze darted around. Above the surface, I could hear Noah yelling at the dehaians standing near the shore.

Zeke dove through the waves, shifting form in a heartbeat and pulling up beside me.

"Why–" I started. I blinked at the sound of my own voice, as clear beneath the water as in the open air. "Why can't I breathe up there?"

A wince twisted his face. "It's not permanent. But the Sylphaen–"

"The who?"

"Those guys who injected that stuff into you. They gave you some messed-up form of neiphiandine. It's a medicine, normally. It forces a full transformation and keeps you like that for a while."

At my expression, he grimaced. "I told you, it's not permanent. But it means you can't go back above the water right now."

"How long does it last?"

Zeke hesitated. "I'm not sure. Depending on what they did to it…"

I exhaled sharply, looking up at Noah.

He was watching me, his face tight with pain.

"So what do I do?" I asked Zeke, not taking my eyes from Noah.

He paused. "Come back with me. My people have doctors. They can take care of you. Fix whatever damage the Sylphaen's drug did."

I turned back, staring at him.

"We can help, Chloe."

My gaze dropped to the sand beneath me. Of their own accord, my hands and tail moved, keeping me balanced in the water.

It wouldn't be forever. It wouldn't even be for a day if I had anything to do with it.

And then I'd come back.

My gaze moved to Noah.

And I'd stay.

I drew a quick breath and then my tail propelled me upward. With a splash, my head broke the surface again and my arms moved instinctively, holding me above the waves.

"Chloe," Noah started, forging through the water toward me. He caught my shoulders, keeping me near him.

"I'm not leaving," I told him, struggling not to wince at the burn of the air on my skin. "Not forever. I… it's just for a little while. Till the drug goes away."

Noah stared at me. "They say there's no telling how long that'll take. After what those bastards gave you…"

I shook my head, gasping at the dense air. "It won't be that bad," I insisted. "You'll see."

He nodded, and then let me go. I dropped beneath the surface, drawing a grateful breath.

"Chloe!" I heard him yell.

I propelled myself back up, and his hands caught me again as I broke the surface. His eyes searched my face as though memorizing it, coming to rest at last on my mouth.

And he drew me close, pressing his warm lips to mine.

My eyes closed. His hands slipped around my back, sending tingles of a whole new kind through my skin and making everything but the feeling of him against me fade away. Desperately, I leaned into him, never wanting him to let go. Beneath his chest, I could feel his heart pounding, his pulse almost as fast as mine.

And then gently, he pulled away.

"Be careful," he told me quietly.

I couldn't respond.

"Go," he said. "Before it starts to hurt too much up here."

He released me, and my hands moved through the water, holding me steady as I trembled with the desire to stay.

"Go, Chloe," he repeated tightly.

"It won't be long," I whispered.

He nodded.

I stared at him for a heartbeat, tears stinging my eyes and the air burning on my skin. And then I spun, diving back into the waves.

Saltwater washed over me, taking only the ache of the air away, and past the surface, I could see Noah looking at me.

He nodded again.

I echoed the motion and then glanced over.

Zeke was watching us.

"Not forever," I said, my voice choked.

"Yeah," he agreed.

The other dehaians dove beneath the waves and swam past us. His brow furrowing, Zeke hesitated and then followed.

I looked back up at Noah. Through the blur of the waves, he smiled.

The pain of leaving crushing down on me, I turned and fled after Zeke into the deep.

Want to know what happens next?

Read Descend
Book two of the Awakened Fate series

Find out about new releases

Join my new release mailing list at skyemalone.com

Loved the book?

Awesome! Would you like to leave a review? Visit Amazon,
Goodreads, or any other book-related site and tell people about it!

Other titles

The Awakened Fate series

The Children and the Blood trilogy (published under the name
Megan Joel Peterson)

About the author

Skye Malone is a fantasy author, which means she spends most of
her time not-quite-convinced that the things she imagines couldn't
actually exist. Born and raised in central Illinois, she hopes someday
to travel the world — though in the meantime she'll take any story
that whisks her off to a place where the fantastic lives inside the
everyday. She loves strong and passionate characters, complex
villains, and satisfying endings that stay with you long after the
book is done. An inveterate writer, she can't go a day without
getting her hands on a keyboard, and can usually be found typing
away while she listens to all the adventures unfolding in her head.

Connect with me

Website: www.skyemalone.com
Twitter: twitter.com/Skye_Malone
Facebook: facebook.com/authorskyemalone
Google Plus: plus.google.com/+SkyeMaloneAuthor

ACKNOWLEDGMENTS

Many thanks are owed to the wonderful people who have supported me in the creation of this story.

To my family and friends, thank you as always for your encouragement.

To Vicki Brown, thank you for beta-reading and for your excitement over the series.

To Tarra Peterson, thank you for your thoughts and input, and for sharing your wonderful enthusiasm about this story as well.

To my mother and sister, Mary Ann and Keri Offenstein, thank you for reassuring me that I wasn't crazy in taking on a mermaid adventure.

To my husband, Eugene, thank you for discussing countless plot points, reading, editing and formatting – and for making sure I actually ate food from time to time, in between writing this story.

And to everyone who has helped spread the word about this book, thank you as well. You all are a gift and I'm deeply grateful for the support.